"I'm taking the baby for the rest of the afternoon."

"Nay, this isn't right. She's my responsibility."

"Don't be stubborn and prideful, Joseph. Baby Leah is going to spend the day with me, and when you come to pick her up, we'll talk about my salary."

"What salary?" He couldn't keep up with her conversational jumps. His mind was a complete fog.

"The one you will pay me to be Leah's nanny."

"I thought you didn't want to do that."

"I've changed my mind. I'll see you later. Have a nice rest. I suggest you lie down on the sofa. That way your neck won't be so stiff."

He opened his mouth to reply. There was some argument he needed to make, but he couldn't summon the wits to figure out what it was. He heard the door close, and silence filled the house. Blessed silence.

Leah was being looked after. Anne could take care of her better than he could.

Anne with the sweet laugh and funny smile who hated his goats and threw tomatoes at him.

After thirty-five years as a nurse, **Patricia Davids** hung up her stethoscope to become a full-time writer. She enjoys spending her free time visiting her grandchildren, doing some long-overdue yard work and traveling to research her story locations. She resides in Wichita, Kansas. Pat always enjoys hearing from her readers. You can visit her online at patriciadavids.com.

Books by Patricia Davids

Love Inspired

Lancaster Courtships

The Amish Midwife

The Amish Bachelors

An Amish Harvest

Brides of Amish Country

An Amish Christmas
The Farmer Next Door
The Christmas Quilt
A Home for Hannah
A Hope Springs Christmas
Plain Admirer
Amish Christmas Joy
The Shepherd's Bride
The Amish Nanny
An Amish Family Christmas: A Plain Holiday
An Amish Christmas Journey
Amish Redemption

Visit the Author Profile page at Harlequin.com for more titles.

The Amish Midwife

USA TODAY Bestselling Author

Patricia Davids

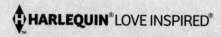

HARLEQUIN® LOVE INSPIRED®

Recycling programs for this product may not exist in your area.

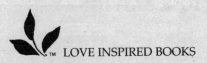

LOVE INSPIRED BOOKS

ISBN-13: 978-0-373-81871-6

The Amish Midwife

www.Harlequin.com

Printed in U.S.A.

Therefore God dealt well with the midwives:
and the people multiplied, and waxed very mighty.
—*Exodus* 1:20

This book is dedicated with great respect to my nephew's wife, Terrah Stroda, a nurse midwife, wife and mother. She has seen the works of God as few people do. May He continue to bless her and her family. I wish to thank my brother, Greg Stroda, for his invaluable information on pumpkin farming. Thanks, bro. Couldn't have done this without you. And I want to extend a special thanks to Te'Coa Seibert for letting me tour her goat dairy and meet her remarkable animals up close. They were too cute. And the fresh cheese was great!

Chapter One

"You miserable *alt gayse*. Oh, no, you don't. Not again!" Anne Stoltzfus shot to her feet when she spotted the intruder working his way under the fence beyond her red barn. She stepped closer to the kitchen window. He was almost through.

"What's wrong?" Roxann Shield remained seated at Anne's kitchen table, her eyes wide with concern.

"It's Joseph Lapp's old goat. He's getting into my garden. I'm not going to lose the last of my precious tomatoes or another prized pumpkin to that thief."

Anne dashed out into the cool morning. Flying down the steps, she raced toward the rickety fence separating her garden plots from her cantankerous neighbor's farm, yelling as she ran. "Out! Get out of there!"

Her nemesis was halfway under the fence when she reached him. Armed with only a kitchen towel, she flew into battle, flapping her weapon in the black-and-brown billy goat's face. The culprit tried to retreat, but his curved horns snagged in the sagging wire. The more he struggled to escape her attack, the more tangled he became. He bleated his misery as loud as he could.

Anne stopped flapping when she recognized his dilemma. He couldn't go forward and he couldn't go back. She rested her hands on her hips as she scowled at him. She heard laughter behind her. Looking over her shoulder, she saw Roxann doubled over with mirth on her front steps.

Anne turned her attention back to the goat. "I should leave you here. It would serve you right to spend the night with your head stuck in the fence."

Feeling sorry for the goat was the last thing she wanted to do, but he did appear miserable sprawled on his belly with his head cocked at an awkward angle. His eyes were wide with fear and his mouth hung open. She looked about for his owner, but Joseph Lapp was nowhere to be seen. Of course he wasn't. Trust her neighbor to be absent when his animal was misbehaving. That was usually the case.

How many times had his goats managed to get in her garden and eat her crops? More than she cared to count. More than she could afford to lose. Each time she drove them out, she bit her tongue to keep from telling Joseph Lapp exactly what she thought of his smelly horde. Her Amish faith required that she forgive grievances, but enough was enough. If the man didn't repair his fences soon, she was going to have a word with Bishop Andy about Joseph's poor stewardship. She didn't want to cause trouble, but she was tired of being on the losing end of the situation.

However satisfying a conversation with the bishop might be, it didn't solve her current problem. The goat continued bleating pitifully. A number of other goats looked over their pens to see what was going on. Anne waited for Joseph to appear, but he didn't. She studied the billy goat for a long moment.

"If you are to be free, I reckon I'll have to do it. Remember this kindness and stay out of my garden."

"Be careful," Roxann called out.

Crouching in front of the goat, Anne put her hand on his head and pushed down so she could untangle his horns. She wrinkled her nose at his stench. Why did he smell so bad? If she had a garden hose handy, she would bathe him before she let him up. Maybe that would deter him from visiting next time. He struggled harder but she was only able to unhook one horn. "Hold still, you wicked animal."

Suddenly, the goat surged forward. His second horn popped free and he made a break for it, barreling into Anne. The impact toppled her backward into her precious tomato plants. Although it was mid-October, the vines still bore huge red fruit, the very last of the summer's bounty and a sure cash crop at her produce stand. She sat in openmouthed shock as the feeling of squished tomatoes beneath her soaked through her dress. So much for a goat's gratitude.

She shook her fist at him. "You miserable, ungrateful beast!"

"Do you need a hand?"

The mildly amused voice came from the far side of the fence. Joseph Lapp stood with his arms crossed on his chest and one hand cupped over his mouth.

He was a tall, brawny man with wide shoulders and muscular arms. A straw hat pulled low on his brow covered his light blond hair. The wide brim cast a shadow across his gray eyes, but she knew he was laughing at her. Again. They rarely shared a conversation, but he was always finding some amusement at her expense. Did he enjoy seeing her suffer?

She scrambled to her feet. "I don't need a hand. I need you to keep your goats out of my garden. Unless you keep them in, I'm going to complain to the bishop."

Joseph walked to the gate between their properties a few yards away and opened it. "Do what you must. Chester, *koom.*"

The billy goat snatched a mouthful of pumpkin leaves and trotted toward the gate. He walked placidly through the opening, but Anne saw the gleam in his beady black eyes when he looked over his shoulder at her. He would be back. Well, she wouldn't be so kind to him next time. It wouldn't be a kitchen towel. She'd find a stout stick.

Joseph closed and latched the gate. "I will

pay for the tomatoes. Just throw the ruined ones over the fence."

She brushed off her stained maroon dress and glared at him. "I'm not going to reward that mangy animal with my fresh tomatoes, even if they are ruined. He'll only come back wanting more."

"Suit yourself. If I can't have them, I won't pay for them."

"Are you serious?" Her mouth dropped open in shock. She took a step toward him and planted her bare foot in another tomato. The pulp oozed between her toes.

"You sat on them. Chester didn't." Joseph turned to walk away.

Furious, Anne plucked the closest whole tomato and threw it with all her might. It hit Joseph squarely between the shoulder blades, splattering in a bright red blob where his suspenders crossed his white shirt.

Horrified, she pressed her hands to her mouth. She had actually hit the man.

Joseph flexed his shoulders. Bits of broken tomato dropped to the ground. Chester jumped on the treats and gobbled them up. Joseph turned to glare at Anne.

She didn't wait to hear what he had to say.

She fled to the house as fast as her shaky legs could carry her. She dashed past Roxann and stopped in the center of her kitchen with her hands pressed to her cheeks.

"What a great throw." Roxann came in, still chuckling. "Did you see the look on his face?"

"In all the years I played baseball as a *kinner*, no one wanted me on their team. I couldn't hit the broad side of the barn when I threw a ball. But today I struck my neighbor."

"You didn't hurt him with a tomato."

"You don't understand." How could she? Roxann was *Englisch*. She didn't have to live by the strict rules of Anne's Amish faith.

Roxann stopped giggling. "Will you get into trouble for it? I know the Amish practice non-violence, but you weren't trying to hurt him."

"I struck him in anger. That is not permitted. *Ever.* If Joseph goes to the bishop or to the church elders, it will be cause for a scandal. I'm so ashamed."

Roxann slipped her arm over Anne's shoulder. "I'm sure Mr. Lapp will forgive you. You are only human. Put it out of your mind and let's finish these reports. You and the other Amish midwives are doing a wonderful job. Your statistics will help me show the administration at my hospital that our outreach education program is paying off. Our funding is running out soon. If we're going to continue educating midwives and the public, we have to prove the benefits outweigh the cost."

Roxann, a nurse-midwife and educator, was determined to improve relations between the medical community and the Amish midwives, who were considered by some doctors to be unskilled and untrained. It was far from the truth.

Anne allowed her mentor and friend to lead her back to the table and resume the review of Anne's cases for the year. Glancing out the kitchen window, Anne looked for Joseph, but he wasn't in sight. She nibbled on her bottom lip. Was he going to make trouble for her?

A full harvest moon, a bright orange ball the color of Anne's pumpkins, was creeping over the hills to the east. The sight made Joseph smile as he closed the barn door after finishing his evening milking. It had been two days since the tomato incident, but he still found himself chuckling at the look on Anne's face when she'd realized what she'd done. From shock to horror to mortification, her expressive features had displayed it all. She might be an annoying little woman, but she did provide him with some entertainment. Especially where his goats were concerned. Her plump cheeks would flush bright red and her green-gray eyes would flash with green fire when she chased his animals. She was no match against their nimbleness, but that didn't keep her from trying.

Goats enjoyed getting out of their pens. Some of them were masters of the skill. Was it his fault that the best forage around was in her garden plot?

It wasn't his intention to make life harder for the woman. He planned to mend his fence, but there simply weren't enough hours in the day. Now that the harvest was done, his corn cribs were full and his hay was safe in the barn, he would find time to make the needed repairs. Tomorrow for sure.

He was halfway to the house when the lights of a car swung off the road and into his lane. He stopped in midstride. Who could that be? He wasn't expecting anyone. Certainly not one of the *Englisch*.

Most likely, it was someone who had taken a wrong turn on the winding rural Pennsylvania road looking for his neighbor's place. It happened often enough to be irritating. His farm was remote and few cars traveled this way until Anne Stoltzfus had opened her produce stand. Now, with her large hand-painted sign out by the main highway and an arrow pointing this direction, he sometimes saw a line of cars on the road heading to buy her fresh-picked corn, squash and now pumpkins. Since the beginning of October, it seemed every *Englisch* in the countssy wanted to buy pumpkins from her. He would be glad when she closed for the winter.

He didn't resent that Anne earned a living working the soil in addition to being a midwife. He respected her for that. He just didn't like people. Some folks called him a recluse. It didn't matter what they called him as long as they left him alone. He cherished the peace and quiet of his small farm with only his animals for company, but that peace was broken now by the crunching of car tires rolling over his gravel drive. From the barn behind him, he heard several of his goats bleating in curiosity.

Whoever these people were, they should know better than to come shopping at an Amish farm after dark. Anne's stand would be closed until morning. The car rolled to a stop a few feet from him. He raised his hand to block the glare of the headlights. He heard the car door open, but he couldn't see anything.

"Hello, *brooder*."

His heart soared with joy at the sound of that familiar and beloved voice. "Fannie?"

"Ja."

His little sister had come home at last. He had prayed for this day for three long years. Prayed every night before he laid his tired body down. She was never far from his thoughts. Still blinded by the lights, he took a step forward. He wanted to hug her, to make sure she was real and not some dream. "I can't believe it's you. *Gott* be praised."

"It's me, right enough, Joe. Johnny, turn off the lights."

Something in the tone of her voice made Joseph stop. Johnny, whoever he was, did as she asked. Joseph blinked in the sudden darkness. He wanted so badly to hear her say she was home for good. "I knew you would come back. I knew when your *rumspringa* ended, you would give up the *Englisch* life and return. Your heart is Amish. You don't belong in the outside world. You belong here."

"I haven't come back to stay, Joe." The regret in her voice cut his joy to shreds. He heard a baby start to cry.

After few seconds, his eyes adjusted and he could make out Fannie standing beside the open door of the vehicle. The light from inside the car didn't reveal his Amish sister. Instead, he saw an *Englisch* girl with short spiky hair, wearing a tight T-shirt and a short denim skirt. He might have passed her on the street without recognizing her, so different did she look. No Amish woman would be seen in such immodest clothes. It was then he realized she held a baby in her arms.

What was going on?

He had raised Fannie alone after their parents and his fiancée were killed in a buggy and pickup crash. He'd taken care of her from the time she was six years old until she disappeared a week after she turned sixteen, leaving only a note to say she wanted an *Englisch* life. For months afterward, he'd waited for her to return and wondered what he had done wrong. How had he failed her so badly? It had to be his fault.

It was hard to speak for the tightness that

formed in his throat. "If you aren't staying, then why are you here?"

The driver, a young man with black hair and a shiny ring in the side of his nose, leaned toward the open passenger-side door. "Come on, Fannie, we don't have all night. Get this over with."

"Shut up, Johnny. You aren't helping." She took a few steps closer to Joseph. "I need your help, *brooder*. There's no one else I can turn to."

Were those tears on her face? "What help can I give you? I don't have money."

"I don't want your money. I…I want you to meet someone. This is my daughter. Your niece. Her name is Leah. I named her after our mother."

"You have a *bubbel*?" Joseph reeled in shock. He still thought of his sister as a little girl skipping off to school or playing on their backyard swing, not someone old enough to be a mother. He gestured toward the car with a jerk of his head. "Is this man your husband?"

"We're not married yet, but we will be soon," she said in a rush.

"Soon?" Had she come to invite him to the wedding?

"*Ja.* As soon as Johnny gets this great job he has waiting for him in New York. He's a musician and I'm a singer. He has an audition with a big-time group. It could be our lucky break. Just what I need to get my career going."

She looked away and bounced the baby. Something wasn't right. Joseph knew her well enough to know she was hiding something.

Maybe he was being too hard on her. Maybe she was simply ashamed of having a babe out of wedlock and she expected her brother to chastise her.

This wasn't the life he wanted for her, but he was a practical man. It did no good to close the barn door after the horse was gone. He struggled to find the words to comfort her. "If Johnny is the man *Gott* has chosen for you, then you will find a blessed life together."

"Thanks. *Danki.* We will have a good life. You'll see. But in the meantime, I need your help. Johnny has to get to his audition, and I'm going to have surgery. Nothing serious, but I can't keep the baby in the hospital with me." She moved the blanket aside and showed him a cast on her wrist.

"It was an accident," Johnny shouted from inside the car.

"It was," Fannie added quickly, her eyes wide. She nibbled at the corner of her lower lip.

"I did not think otherwise." At least not until this moment. He eyed Johnny sharply. *Nay*, it was wrong of him to think the worst of any man. If his sister said it was an accident, he must believe her. He nodded toward the house. "Come in. We can talk there. I have a pot of *coffe* on the stove."

"No, thanks. Your coffee was always strong enough to dissolve a horseshoe. I can't stay, Joe. Please say you will take care of Leah for me. It's only for a couple of days."

"Think what you are asking. I have no experience with babies."

"You raised me."

"You were not in diapers."

"Please, Joe. If you don't keep her, I don't know what I'll do. I have everything she'll need in a bag for you. I've even mixed a couple of bottles. Keep them in the fridge and warm them in a pan of hot water when you need them. That's all you'll have to do. If you run out, there's powdered formula in here." She set a pink-and-white diaper bag down by her feet.

"Hurry it up, Fan, or I'm going to leave without you." Johnny's snarling tone made her flinch. Joseph scowled at him. Johnny sank back behind the wheel muttering to himself.

Joseph shook his head. Why was she with such a fellow? "This is not a good idea, Fannie. You know I would help if I could."

She moved close to him. "I'm desperate, Joe," she whispered.

Glancing at the car, she kissed the baby's forehead. "She will be safe with you. I won't worry about her for a single minute. Please. I know this sounds crazy, but it's what's best for her." She thrust the baby into his arms and hurried away.

Stunned, Joseph froze and then tried to give the baby back, but his sister was already getting in the car. "Fannie, wait!"

The moonlight showed her tear-streaked face and her hand pressed to the window as the car took off with a spray of gravel. He stood staring after it until the taillights disappeared.

"Don't do this, sister. Come back," he muttered into the darkness.

The baby started crying again.

Chapter Two

Startled awake from a sound sleep, Anne tried to get her bearings. It took her a moment to realize someone was pounding on her front door downstairs.

She threw back the quilt and turned on the battery-operated lantern she kept on her nightstand. As a midwife, she was used to callers in the middle of the night, but only Rhonda Yoder was due soon. Anne lived so far away from them that the plan was for Rhonda's husband to use the community telephone when she was needed. Anne carried a cell phone that had been approved by the bishop for use in emergencies. She checked it. No calls had come in.

After spending the previous day and night delivering Dora Stoltzfus's first child, Anne was so tired it was hard to think straight. Maybe Dora or the baby was having trouble.

The knocking downstairs started again.

"I'm coming." After covering her head with a white kerchief, she pulled on her floor-length pink robe, making sure her long brown braid was tucked inside.

She hurried down the stairs, opened the door and gazed with sleep-heavy eyes at the man standing on her front porch. She blinked twice to make sure she wasn't dreaming and held the lantern higher. "Joseph?"

Why was her neighbor pounding on her door at two o'clock in the morning? He shifted a bundle he held in the crook of his arm. "I require your help, woman."

That didn't make any sense. Joseph was a confirmed bachelor who lived alone. "You need the services of a midwife?"

"That is why I'm here." He spoke as if she were slow-witted. Maybe she was. What was going on?

It had been almost a week since she'd hit him with a tomato. This wasn't his way of getting back at her, was it? Suddenly, the most probable answer occurred to her.

She reared back to glare at him. "Don't tell

me it's for one of your goats. I'm not a vet, Joseph Lapp."

She was ready to shut the door in his face. Joseph's passion was his annoying goats. They were practically family to him. He preferred their company to that of his human neighbors. She often saw him walking in the pastures with the herd surrounding him. The frolicking baby kids were cute in the springtime, but it was the adults, Chester in particular, who saw her garden as a free salad bar.

"She's sick and I don't know what's wrong." The bundle Joseph held began whimpering. He lifted the corner of the blanket and uncovered a baby's face.

Anne's stared in openmouthed surprise. Her lantern highlighted the worry lines around his eyes as he looked at the infant he held. This wasn't a prank. He wasn't joking.

"Joseph, what are you doing with a *bubbel*? Where's her *mudder*?" The babe looked to be only a few months old.

"Gone."

"Gone where? Who is the *mudder*?" None of this made sense. Anne felt like she was caught in a bad dream.

"It's Fannie's child."

"Fannie?"

"My sister."

Anne had heard that Joseph's sister had left the Amish years ago. It had broken his heart, or so everyone said. Anne wasn't sure he had a heart to begin with.

"Can you help her?"

His terse question galvanized her into action. He had a sick child in his arms and he had come to her for help. She stepped away from the door. "Come in. How long has the babe been ill? Does she have a fever?"

Shouldering past Anne, he entered the house. "She has been fussy since her mother left her with me four nights ago, but it got worse this morning. No fever, but she throws up everything I've given her to drink. Tonight she wouldn't stop crying. She has a rash now, too."

The crying was more of a pitiful whimper. "Bring her into my office."

Anne led the way to a small room off the kitchen where she met with her mothers-to-be for checkups and did well-baby exams on the infants as they grew. She quickly lit a pair of gas lanterns, bathing the space in light. She pulled her midwife kit, a large black leather satchel, off the changing table and said, "Put her down here."

He did but he kept one hand on the baby in case she rolled over. At least he knew a little about babies. That was something of a surprise, too, in this night of surprises. His worry deepened the creases on his brow. Sympathy for him stirred inside her.

Joseph Lapp was a loner. He was a member of her Amish congregation, but he wasn't close friends with anyone she knew about. When there was trouble in the community or someone in need, he came and did his part, but he never stayed to socialize, something that was as normal as breathing to most of the Amish she knew. He didn't shun people. He just seemed to prefer being alone.

They had been neighbors for almost three years and this was the first time he had been inside her home. A big man, he stood six foot two, if not more, with broad shoulders and hammer-like fists. He towered over Anne and made the small room feel even smaller. She took hold of the baby and tried to ignore his overwhelming presence. He took a step back, thrust his hands in his pockets and hunched his shoulders as if he felt the tightness, too.

Anne quickly unwrapped and examined the little girl. The baby was thin and pale with dark hollows around her eyes. She looked like she didn't feel good. "How old is she?"

"I don't know for certain."

This was stranger and stranger. "I would guess three or four months. She's a little dehydrated and she is clearly in pain." The baby kept drawing her knees up and whimpering every few minutes. The sides of her snug faded yellow sleeper were damp. It was a good sign. If the baby was wet, that meant she wasn't seriously dehydrated.

"She needs changing, for one thing. Do you have a clean diaper?" Anne glanced at him.

"At the house, not with me."

"There are some disposable diapers in the white cabinet on the wall. Bring me one and a box of baby wipes, too."

He jumped to do as she requested. Anne took off the sleeper that was a size too small as well as the dirty diaper, noting a bright red rash on the baby's bottom. "Bring me that blue tube of cream, too."

When Joseph handed her the things she'd asked for, she quickly cleaned the child, applied a thick layer of aloe to the rash and

secured a new diaper in place. It didn't stop
the baby's whimpering as she had hoped. She
carefully checked the little girl over, looking
for other signs of illness or injury.

Joseph shifted from foot to foot. "Do you
know what's wrong with her?"

Perplexed, Anne shook her head. She didn't
want to jump to a faulty conclusion. "I'm not
sure. Her belly is soft. She doesn't have a fever
or any bruising. I don't see anything other than
a mild diaper rash and a baby who clearly
doesn't feel well. I reckon it could be a virus.
Is anyone else in the family sick?"

"I'm fine."

Anne wrapped the baby in her blanket, lifted
the child to her shoulder and turned to face Joseph. "What about her *mudder*?"

"I don't think so. She wasn't sick when i
saw her last, but I only spoke to her for a few
minutes."

The baby began sucking noisily on her fingers. Anne studied the child as she considered
what to do next. A cautious course seemed the
best move. "She acts hungry. I have some electrolyte solution I'd like to give her. It's water
with special additives to help children with

sick stomachs. Let's see if she can keep a little of that down. What's her name?"

"Leah."

"*Hallo*, Leah," Anne crooned to the child and then handed the baby to Joseph. He took her gingerly, clearly unused to holding one so little. The babe looked tiny next to his huge hands.

Why would Leah's mother leave her baby in the care of a confirmed bachelor like Joseph? It didn't make sense. There were a lot of questions Anne wanted to ask, but first things first. "I need to see if Leah can keep down some fluids. If she can't, we'll have to consider taking her to the nearest hospital."

That would mean a long buggy ride in the dark. It wasn't an emergency. An ambulance wasn't needed. Anne glanced at Joseph to gauge his willingness to undertake such a task. He nodded his consent. "I will do what you think is best."

He put the baby's welfare above his own comfort. That was good. Her estimation of his character went up a notch. "Let's hope it doesn't come to that. I'll put the wet sleeper in a plastic bag for you. It's too small for her, anyway."

"It's the only clothing she has." He gently rocked the child in his arms.

"Nothing else?"

"*Nay*, just diapers."

"She's been wearing the same sleeper for four days?"

His eyes flashed to Anne's, a scowl darkening his brow. "I washed it."

Why wouldn't Leah's mother leave him clothes for the child? That was odd and odder yet. A baby could go through a half-dozen changes a day between spitting up and messing their diapers. "I have some baby clothes you can take home with you. I buy them at yard sales and people give them to me so I have some for mothers who can't afford clothing." Not all of her mothers were Amish. She had delivered two dozen *Englisch* babies during her time in Honeysuckle. The clothes had come in handy for several of the poorer women.

Anne pulled open a lower cabinet door and gave Joseph a pink gown from her stash of baby clothes. She put several sleepers and T-shirts in a spare diaper bag for him, too.

He dressed Leah while Anne fixed a few ounces of electrolyte water in a bottle. When it was ready, Anne took Leah from him and settled in a rocker in the corner. He took a seat in a ladder-back chair on the opposite side of the room. He leaned forward and braced his massive arms on his thighs. Even seated, he took up more room than most men. Her office had never felt so cramped.

The baby sucked eagerly, clutching the bottle and holding it while watching Anne with wide blue eyes. Leah belched without spitting up and smiled around the rubber nipple, making Anne giggle. What a cutie she was with her big eyes and wispy blond hair.

Anne stole a glance at Joseph. He had flaxen hair, too, cut in the usual bowl style that Amish men wore. It was straight as wheat straw except for the permanent crease his hat made over his temples. His eyes weren't blue, though. They were gray. As dark as winter storm clouds. When coupled with his dour expression, they were enough to chill the friendliest overture.

Not that she and Joseph were friendly neighbors. The only time she saw him other than church was when she was chasing after his miserable, escape-happy goats and trying to drive them out of her garden, while he was laughing at her from the other side of the fence. He didn't laugh out loud, but she had seen the smirk on his face. She thought he secretly enjoyed watching her run after his animals. "How are your goats, Joseph?"

He frowned. "What?"

"Your goats. How are they? They haven't been in my garden for days."

A twitch at the corner of his mouth could have been the start of a smile, but she wasn't sure. "They're fine. I reckon they got tired of you flapping your apron or your towels at them and decided to stay home for a spell."

"Or it could be because I fixed the hole in your fence."

He looked surprised. "Did you? I'm grateful. I've been meaning to get to that. How is she doing?"

Anne looked at the quiet baby in her arms and smiled. The scowl on the baby's face was gone. She blinked owlishly. "She's trying to stay awake, but her eyelids are growing heavier by the minute. She seems fine right now. All we can do is wait and see if she keeps this down."

He let out a heavy sigh. "At least she isn't crying. It near broke my heart to listen to her."

So he did have a heart, and a tender one, at

that. Her estimation of his character went up another notch.

"You said this started this morning. Was there anything different? Do you think she could have put something in her mouth without you seeing it?"

"I don't think so."

"Has there been a change in her food? Did you make sure and boil the water before mixing her formula?' Most of the Amish farms had wells. Without testing, it was impossible to tell if the water was safe for an infant to drink. She always advised boiling well water.

"*Ja.* I followed the directions on the can I bought yesterday. Her mother left me some mixed bottles, but I went through them already. The can of powdered formula in the bag was nearly empty."

"You bought a new can of formula? Did you get the same brand?" That might account for the upset stomach.

He shrugged. "I think so. Aren't they all alike?'

"Not really."

"She hasn't spit up your fancy water. She seems fine now. *Danki.*"

Anne gazed tenderly at the babe in her

arms. Babies were all so precious. Each and every one was a blessing. Times like this always brought a pang of pain to her heart. She wished her baby had survived. Even though she had been only seventeen and pregnant out of wedlock, she would have loved her little boy with all her heart.

But God had other plans for their lives. He'd called her son home before he had a chance to draw a breath here on earth. She didn't understand it, but she had to follow the path He laid out even if it didn't include motherhood.

She refused to feel sorry for herself. She would hold her son in Heaven when her time came. She loved her job as a midwife and she was grateful she could help bring new life into the world and comfort families when things went wrong. Her own tragedy left her well suited to understand a mother's grief.

Anne stroked the baby's cheek. "She does seem to be better, but let's give it an hour or so before we celebrate."

"One less hour of sleep is fine with me as long as you don't mind."

Anne looked up, surprised that he would consider her comfort when he looked as tired and worn out as she felt. She had never seen him looking so worried. "Where is Fannie? Why did she leave Leah with you?"

He was silent for so long that Anne thought he wasn't going to tell her anything. He stared at his clasped hands and finally spoke. "Fannie brought the baby to me four days ago. She said she had to have surgery and couldn't keep the child with her in the hospital. She asked me to watch her for a few days."

"What about the baby's father? Why couldn't he watch the child?"

"He had to get to New York for a job interview."

"Which hospital is she in?"

"She didn't say. She'll be back soon. Probably this morning."

"It seems strange that she didn't tell you which hospital she was going to. Did she leave a phone number or a way to contact her?"

He rose to his feet. "I should go. It's not right that I'm here alone with you. I'm sorry. I wasn't thinking straight. If the bishop hears of this, it could mean trouble for you. You have your reputation to protect."

"I'm sure Bishop Andy would understand. You were only thinking of the baby."

Speaking of the bishop reminded Anne of

her regretful behavior toward Joseph. "I want to beg your forgiveness for my grave lapse in manners the other day. I've never done anything like that before. I'm humiliated and so very sorry that I acted as I did. You would be within your rights to report me to the church elders for discipline."

"It's forgiven. The babe seems fine now. *Danki.* I should go home." He reached for the baby, and Anne let him take her.

"Feed her the electrolyte water if she wakes up hungry again tonight. Tomorrow you can mix a little formula with it. One part milk to three parts water. If she tolerates that, mix it half and half for the next feeding."

"I understand. *Guten nacht*, Anne. You've been a great help. I appreciate the loan of the clothes, too."

"Tell Fannie she can keep them if she wants. Good night, Joseph," Anne called after him, but he was already out the door.

Was he that concerned about her reputation or was he reluctant to answer any more questions about his sister? At least he had forgiven her for striking him. That was a relief. Shaking her head over the whole thing, Anne put out the lights and climbed the stairs to bed for what was left of her night.

Waking at her usual time, Anne fixed a pot of strong coffee and made her plans for the day. She didn't have any mother's visits scheduled, so her whole day could be devoted to getting her pumpkins up to her roadside stand. After two cups and some toast, she was ready to get to work.

Outside, she took her old wheelbarrow out to her patch and began loading it with ripe pumpkins. Her white ones and the traditional orange carving pumpkins were her bestsellers, but she did have a number of cooking pumpkins ready to be picked. She added three of them to the top of the heap in her wheelbarrow for her own use. Having planted a new cooking variety, she was anxious to see if they were as good as her tried-and-true heirloom ones.

A crooked front wheel made pushing the wheelbarrow a chore, but getting it fixed would have to wait. If she came out ahead on her produce stand this fall, she was definitely investing in a new pushcart. Leaving the barrow at the front steps, she carried her cooking pumpkins in and put them in the sink to be washed.

She stood contemplating another cup of coffee when she heard someone shouting her name.

She opened the front door. Joseph came sprinting toward her with Leah in his arms.

Chapter Three

"Joseph, what's wrong?" Anne held the door wide for him.

He rushed inside looking frazzled and more exhausted than the last time she had seen him. "I did as you told me. She was fine the rest of the night. When I gave her some of the formula this morning, she threw up again and her face got all blotchy. Now she won't stop crying."

Anne could see that for herself. Joseph's blue shirt had a large wet streak down the front. The unmistakable odor of sour milk emanated from him. Leah continued to wail. It was hard to tell if she was red in the face from crying or from something else. Anne began to suspect the child had an intolerance to milk.

She took the baby from him, sat down in a kitchen chair and unwrapped the blanket

Leah was swaddled in. The baby was wearing the long pink gown that Anne had given Joe last night. She untied the ribbon from around the hem and pulled up the material, exposing Leah's kicking legs and belly and more red blotches. Anne had seen this kind of reaction before and was almost sure she was right. "I think she may have an allergy to the formula."

He shook his head. "I checked the can her mother gave me. It's the same brand I got for her. How can a baby be allergic to milk?"

"Some babies just are." It was possible the rash was from something else, but it seemed too coincidental that it appeared immediately after she'd had the formula. Anne needed more information.

Joseph ran a hand through his hair. "She can't live on water."

"*Nay*, she can't." Anne pulled the gown down and wrapped the blanket loosely around her. Lifting the baby to her shoulder, she patted the fussy child's back until she quieted.

"Then what do I feed her?" Joseph sounded like a man at the end of his rope. Looking as if he hadn't slept a wink, he raked a hand through his disheveled hair again. He hadn't bothered putting on his hat. If Anne needed proof of how upset he was, she had it. Joseph never left his house without his straw hat unless it was to wear his black felt hat to Sunday services.

She shifted the baby to the crook of her arm. "You may need to switch her to a soy formula. I need to know what brand you gave her. It could be that you just need a different kind of milk."

"I'll get it." He rushed out of the house, leaped off the porch without touching the steps and sprinted toward his home a few hundred yards to the south. Anne watched as he vaulted the fence at the edge of his property instead of using the gate and kept running. She didn't know a man his size could move so fast.

She struggled not to laugh as she gazed at Leah. "You're certainly showing me a different side of my neighbor. Do be kinder to the poor man. I think he's having a hard time adjusting to you."

It was clear that Joseph was deeply concerned about his niece and determined to do whatever it took to help her. Anne watched him rush into his house and wondered what else she would learn about Joseph Lapp while he cared for his niece.

Did his sister have any idea how much she

had disrupted her brother's life? Anne didn't know Fannie, but she found it hard to picture anyone leaving a baby with Joseph, even for a few days. Still, his sister would know him better than Anne did. She'd seen him bottle-feeding young goats in his pen. Maybe he knew more about infants than she gave him credit for knowing.

Leah buried her face against Anne's chest and began rubbing it back and forth. She whimpered and then started crying again, pulling Anne's attention away from her thoughts of Joseph.

Anne stroked the baby's head. "You poor little thing. That rash itches, doesn't it? I have something I think will help."

Joseph came sprinting into Anne's house and skidded to a stop on her black-and-white-patterned linoleum. The baby had stopped screaming. Leah sat naked, splashing and giggling in a basin of water in the center of the kitchen table. Anne cooed to the child as she supported her and poured a cupful of the liquid over her slick little body. Leah wagged her arms up and down in delight.

He took a couple of gasping breaths and held

out the cans. "This is what I gave her and this is what her mother left me."

"Just set them on the table." Anne didn't even look at him. She was grinning foolishly at the baby and making silly noises. Leah seemed mesmerized by Anne's mouth and the sounds she was making.

He put the new formula on the tabletop along with the empty can he'd pulled from the trash. Thankfully, he'd been too busy to burn his barrel yesterday. He dropped onto a chair as he waited for his racing heart to slow. It seemed his mad dash was for nothing. Both Anne and Leah were enjoying the bathing process. He soon noticed the communication they seemed to share.

Leah was attempting to mimic the shape of Anne's mouth. When Anne opened her mouth wide, Leah did, too. When Anne pursed her lips together, Leah tried to imitate her. Although the baby couldn't produce the sounds Anne was making, it was clear she was trying to do so. She flapped her arms in excitement.

After a few minutes, Joseph realized he was staring at Anne's mouth, too. She had full red lips that tilted up slightly at the corners in a perpetual sweet smile. He liked her smile.

He hadn't paid much attention to her in the past but now he noticed her sable-brown hair glinted with gold highlights where it wasn't covered by her white *kapp*. It was thick and healthy looking.

She was a little woman. The top of her head wouldn't reach his chin even if she stood on tiptoe. Apple-cheeked and just a shade on the plump side, she had a cute button nose generously sprinkled with ginger freckles and wide owlish gray-green eyes. She wasn't a beauty, but she had a sweet face. Why hadn't he noticed that about her before? Maybe because he usually saw her when she was running after his goats, when she was furious.

He'd been leery when a single woman moved into the small house next to his. It had been an *Englisch* house before Anne bought it. It took her a while to convert it to meet their Amish rules, but the bishop had been tolerant of her progress because she was single.

She hadn't set her sights on Joseph the way some of the single women in the community had over the years. He wasn't the marrying kind. Apparently, Anne wasn't the marrying kind, either. She had to be close to thirty, if not older. He'd never seen her walking out with any of the unwed men in their Plain community. The only fellow he'd seen hanging around her had been Micah Shetler. He was known as something of a flirt, but she'd never shown any interest in return and Micah had soon stopped coming around.

Anne minded her own business and let Joseph mind his. If it wasn't for the traffic her produce stand brought in and her dislike of his goats, he would have said she was the perfect neighbor. She was proving to be a godsend today. He pulled his gaze away from her and concentrated on Leah. The baby looked happier than he'd seen her since she arrived. "She seems to be enjoying her bath."

"I put some baking soda in the water to soothe her itching skin. It will help for a little while. Grab that towel for me, would you, please?" Anne lifted the baby from the water. Joseph jumped up and held the towel wide. He wrapped it around the baby when Anne handed her to him.

"Should I bathe her this way?" How much baking soda? How often? He didn't want to show his ignorance, so he didn't ask.

"If her rash doesn't go away, you can. We need to find out what is causing the rash in the first place. I'm pretty sure she has an allergy to something."

When he had the baby securely in his arms, Anne picked up the two formula cans. "This is odd."

"Did I buy the wrong thing?"

"*Nay*, it's nothing you did. This is soy formula. It's often used for babies that are sensitive to cow's milk–based formulas. I wish I could ask Fannie why Leah is on it. Was it her first choice, or did the baby have trouble with regular formula and so she switched her to soy? It's puzzling."

"What difference would it make?" He laid the baby and towel on the table and began drying her. She tried to stuff the fingers of both hands in her mouth.

"If Leah had trouble tolerating regular formula, there isn't any point in giving her what I have on hand. Do you or Fannie have a milk allergy?"

"Not that I know of."

Anne stepped up and took over the task of drying and dressing Leah. He happily stood aside.

Leah quickly became dissatisfied with her

fingers and started fussing again. He glanced at Leah. "Have you more of that special water?"

"I do, but I think I want to try something else. Do you have any fresh goat's milk?"

"*Nay*, the truck collected my milk yesterday evening. I haven't milked yet this morning. Are you planning to give her goat's milk?"

"It won't hurt to try it."

He had heard of babies being raised on goat's milk, but he wouldn't have thought of it. "I can bring you some fresh as soon as I catch a goat. How much do you need?"

"A quart to start with. I'll have to cook it first. I don't want to give her raw milk."

He bristled at her insult. He ran a first-class dairy. "My goats have all been tested for disease and are healthy. I have a permit to sell raw milk and my operation is inspected regularly. I drank raw goat's milk when I was growing up and it didn't hurt me."

She looked him up and down. "I can see it didn't stunt your growth. I'm not questioning the sanitation of your dairy. I feel babies shouldn't have raw cow or goat's milk until they are much older than Leah is. I grew up drinking raw milk, too."

"Cow's milk? Maybe that's what stunted your growth."

"Very funny," she snapped, but he detected a sparkle of humor in her eyes.

He folded his arms over his chest. "You don't like my goats."

"I'm sure they are wonderful animals."

"My does are some of the finest milk producers in the state."

"Joseph, I don't have to like your goats to make a formula from their milk. Let's hope Leah can tolerate it. Are you going to go catch a goat or do I have to?"

"I've seen you herd goats. You'd still be chasing them tomorrow. I'll be back in a few minutes."

"Make sure you use a very clean container to put the milk in."

He shook his head as he walked out of her house. If she knew anything about his work, she would know his pails were stainless steel and cleaned with soap, water and bleach twice a day. He took good care of his animals and his equipment. How could she live next door to him and not know that?

Maybe the same way he'd never noticed how

pretty her smile was. He hadn't been inclined to look closely. Until now.

As he crossed the ground between his house and Anne's, he looked her property over with a critical eye. Some of the siding on her horse barn was loose and the paint was faded. It could use a new coat. The pile of manure outside the barn was overdue for spreading in the fields. Two of the vanes on her windmill clacked as they went around, proving they were loose, too.

He hadn't noticed things were slipping into disrepair for her. He hadn't been a very good neighbor. They were all things he could fix in a day or two. As soon as Fannie came for Leah, he would see to the repairs as a way to thank Anne for her kindness to the baby. It was the least he could do.

When Fannie came back.

She would be back. She was later than she'd said she would be, but he was sure she had a good reason. He just wished he knew what it was. Why hadn't she contacted him? He'd checked the answering machine in the community phone booth out by the highway twice a day for the past two days. He knew she had that number.

Her whispered words, the memory of her tearful face in the car window had flashed into his mind when she didn't return as promised. The pain and sorrow he had seen in her eyes gave rise to a new doubt in his mind. Had she abandoned her child with him? Each passing hour without word made him worry that she might have done so. It wasn't right to suspect her of such a thing, but the doubts wouldn't be silenced.

As always, his goats were happy to see him and frolicked in their pens as he approached. In spite of what Anne thought, his goats were all as tame as kittens. They came when he called them, with Matilda, the oldest female, leading all the others in a group behind her. He selected Jenny from the milling animals and opened the gate leading to his milking barn.

"Jenny, up you go."

The brown-and-black doe knew the routine. She trotted up the ramp onto the waist-high platform and put her head in the stanchion. He gave her a handful of alfalfa hay and closed the bar that would keep her from pulling her head out if she was finished eating before he was finished milking her. He didn't bother hooking her to his milking machine. His church allowed the limited use of electricity in some Amish businesses such as Joseph's dairy. The electric milking machines and refrigeration allowed him to sell his milk as Grade A to *Englisch* customers for more money. Today he milked Jenny by hand. In less than five minutes, he had a frothing pailful of milk.

After giving Jenny a quick scratch behind the ear to let her know he was pleased, he opened the head lock and allowed her to rejoin the herd. Holding the pail high, he waded through the group of younger goats vying for his attention and went out the gate before making sure it was latched securely. They bleated until he was out of sight.

The sound of a car on the road caught his attention. He looked hopefully toward the end of his lane, but it was only the mailman. The white truck stopped at Joseph's box.

Maybe there would be a letter from his sister explaining everything. He put down the pail and strode toward his mailbox at the end of the drive. He refused to think about how many times he'd made this trip praying to find a missive from her in the past. She didn't have a baby then. She had to be concerned about her child.

The mail carrier drove away before Joseph reached him, but he didn't care. He wasn't in the mood to visit with the talkative fellow. Opening his mailbox, Joseph pulled out a bundle of envelopes and flyers. Leafing through them, he found they were advertisements and junk mail until he reached the final envelope.

Immediately, he recognized his sister's handwriting, although he hadn't seen it in years. The letter was addressed to Joe Lapp. For some reason, she insisted on calling him Joe, when no one else did. Relieved, he tore open the letter and asked God's forgiveness for doubting his sister. As he read, his relief turned to disbelief.

When Joseph entered Anne's kitchen, he presented the pail of milk to her without a word. He had a strange dejected look on his face. Had one of his beloved goats kicked him? Knowing how much he'd been through, she decided not to tease him about it.

She gave him the baby to hold and took the pail to her stove. Their Amish church allowed members to use propane-powered appliances in the home. Her hot-water heater, refrigerator, washer, stove and some of her lighting all ran off propane.

Anne transferred the milk to a large kettle. "It will take a while to heat this through. She got fussy when you left, so I gave her some more electrolyte solution. I can bring the formula to your house when I'm finished."

Anne glanced at him. He held Leah close, gazing intently at her face. He rubbed his eye with the back of his hand and sniffed.

"Is something wrong, Joseph?"

"Nay."

She could see that wasn't true, but she didn't press him. She glanced covertly at him as she went back to measuring and mixing ingredients together. She referred frequently to a paper on the counter beside her. Her mother had come up with a goat's milk formula years earlier after consulting with a local doctor. Anne was grateful for her mother's thorough record keeping. She added molasses to a glass measuring cup that held a small amount of coconut oil. It didn't look appetizing. "Have you had breakfast, Joseph?"

He cleared his throat. "I'm fine. You go ahead."

She looked his way and noticed he was staring at her concoction. She grinned. "This isn't breakfast, but I could make you some eggs. There is still some coffee in the pot, too."

"Just the *coffe* sounds good. What is it that you're making?"

"Formula."

"I thought you were going to give her the goat's milk."

"I am. Goat's milk is perfect for baby goats, but it is lacking some things that a human baby needs. I don't have all the ingredients here, but if she tolerates this milk, I can give you a list of things you'll have to buy."

"Like what?"

"Liquid whey. Molasses or Grade B maple syrup. Cod liver oil and extra-virgin olive oil plus coconut oil and liquid vitamins. There are a few other things, as well."

His frown deepened. "How often will I have to do all this?"

"Every other day at least. The milk needs to be fresh, but it can be kept refrigerated for two days. What I'm making now will last through today unless Leah can't tolerate it. You said Fannie would be back today, didn't you? Send her over when she comes to pick up the baby, and I'll show her how it's made."

"You had best show me how to do it. I'll be the one taking care of her from now on."

Confused, Anne turned to him. "What about her *mudder*? Isn't she coming? What's happened?"

Chapter Four

The anguish on Joseph's face told Anne something was very wrong. She watched him struggle to compose himself. What had happened to his sister?

He sank onto one of her chairs and gazed at the baby for a long time. Finally, he whispered, "Your *mudder* is not coming."

"She's not coming today?" Anne waited for him to elaborate.

He shook his head. "She's not coming back at all."

Anne cupped a hand over her mouth as a horrible thought occurred to her. "She died?"

"*Nay*, but that would be easier to explain."

"Please, Joseph, tell me what has happened."

"Fannie lied to me."

Anne took a seat beside him. "In what way did she lie?"

"When she left Leah with me, she said it would only be for a day or two. She deliberately lied to me."

"I don't understand."

He pulled a letter from his coat pocket. "This came in the mail this morning. It's from Fannie. I was happy when I saw it. I thought it would explain why she was late returning. Instead, she wrote that she didn't have surgery. That was a lie she made up to get me to keep Leah. Fannie was going to New York City with Johnny. She said her baby was better off growing up in the country rather than in the city."

"Oh, Joseph, I'm so sorry." It was clear he was hurting and she didn't know how to help.

He looked at her, his eyes filled with confusion and pain. "What kind of mother would do that? I tried to raise my sister to be a God-fearing woman of faith, but I failed. I don't know what I did wrong. I knew my duty. I kept us fed and together with a roof over our heads. I dried her tears. I took her to church. I made sure she said her prayers. Then she does this, and I think I never knew her at all."

He put the letter away and adjusted the

blanket so it wasn't covering Leah's mouth. "Why couldn't she be happy among us? Is this life so terrible?"

Anne laid a hand on his arm. "We can't know what is in another person's mind or the reasons why they behave as they do, unless they share that with us." Her heart ached for the pain he was going through. He had suffered a terrible betrayal of trust.

"How can I raise another child after I failed so miserably with my sister?"

Anne wished she could offer him the comfort he needed. She searched for the right words. "We do what we must. We depend on *Gottes* grace to see us through. Leah will be a blessing to you."

He pressed his lips into a tight line and shook his head. "*Nay.* She will grow to hate me and abandon her faith as her mother has done."

"You don't know that." He was upset, not thinking straight. Anne didn't blame him. This was a terrible shock.

He surged to his feet. "I know I can't raise a baby. I can't! You know what to do. You take her! You raise her." He thrust Leah toward her. The baby started crying.

Anne jumped out of her chair and backed against the counter as she held up both hands. "Don't say that. She is your niece, your blood. You will find the strength you need to care for her."

"She needs more than my strength. She needs a mother's love. I can't give her that. I couldn't give Fannie that."

Anne covered her eyes with her hands. He had no idea what he was offering. For years after she lost her son, she'd suffered a recurring dream. In it, she found a baby alone in some unlikely place. In the barn or out in the garden. She was always alone, and Anne rejoiced because she could keep the unwanted child. Yet every dream ended exactly the same way. The moment she had the baby in her arms, someone would take it from her. She woke aching with loss all over again.

Joseph had no idea what a precious gift he was trying to give away. He didn't understand the grief he would feel when his panic subsided. She had to make him see that.

Lowering her hands, she stared into his eyes, willing him to understand. "I can help you, Joseph, but I can't raise Leah for you. You're upset. That's understandable. Fannie has wounded you deeply, but she must have enormous faith in you. Think about it. She could have given her child to an *Englisch* couple or another Amish family. She didn't. She wanted Leah to be raised by you, in our Amish ways. Don't you see that?"

He rubbed a hand over his face. "I don't know what to think."

"You're tired. You haven't had much sleep in the past four days. If you truly feel you can't raise Leah, you must go to Bishop Andy and seek his council. He will know what to do."

"He will tell me it is my duty to raise her, just as the bishop before told me it was my duty to raise Fannie. Did you mean it when you said you would help me?" His voice held a desperate edge.

"Of course I meant it. Before you make any rash decisions, let's see if we can get this fussy child to eat something. Nothing wears on the nerves faster than a crying *bubbel* that can't be consoled."

He needed a break. Anne could give him one. It was the least she could do. She took the baby from him.

He raked his hands through his thick blond

hair again. "I must milk my herd and get them fed."

"That's fine, Joseph. Go and do what you must. Leah can stay with me until you're done, but I have to get my pumpkins up to my stand before long. Customers will be arriving soon. It's getting late." It was nearly nine o'clock.

He stepped back and rubbed his hands on the sides of his pants. "I reckon I can take your load of pumpkins up to the roadway for you before I milk."

"That would be *wunderbar*, Joseph. *Danki*. But I should warn you that the front wheel is loose and it wobbles."

He gave her a wry smile. "So do your windmill blades. There are tools to fix those things."

She leveled a hard stare at him. "Are they the same tools you could use to fix a fence so your goats don't get out? What a pity neither one of us owns such wonders."

He had the good grace to look embarrassed. "I may have a few tools lying around somewhere. If you can get Leah to eat without throwing up, I'll fix your wheelbarrow and your windmill."

"I would do it without a bribe, but you have

a deal." At least he seemed calmer. The look of panic had left his eyes.

"*Danki*, Anne Stoltzfus. You have been a blessing. You have proven you are a good neighbor. Something I have not been to you." He went out the door with hunched shoulders, as if he carried the weight of the world upon them.

Anne looked down at Leah. "He'd better come back for you. I know where he lives."

The baby continued to fuss softly, trying to suck on her fingers, trying to catch anything to put in her mouth.

Anne shifted Leah to her hip, freeing one hand to finish mixing the formula, and went to her stove. When she was done with the milk and it had cooled enough, she poured some in a bottle mixed with her electrolyte solution and sat down in the rocker in her office. Leah latched on to the bottle but spat it out and fussed louder.

"Don't be that way. I know it tastes different, but give it a chance." Anne offered the bottle again. Leah began sucking, reluctantly at first, then with gusto. She managed to clasp the bottle in her tiny hands and pulled it closer, hanging on to it for dear life.

"Not so fast. You'll make yourself sick."
Anne took the bottle away. A tiny scowl appeared on Leah's face, reminding Anne of the
one that normally marked Joseph's brow. She
had to smile. "You take after your mother's
side of the family."

What a beautiful child she was. Anne sighed
heavily. "It's not that I don't want you. You
understand that, don't you? To have a babe of
my own, I would love that, but I have stopped
thinking it is possible. I only met one man I
wished to marry and he didn't want to marry
me. I'm not a spring chicken anymore. I'll be
thirty-four in June."

Leah didn't comment, but she was watching Anne intently.

Anne closed her eyes as she rocked the
child. "I stopped having dreams about finding babies when I turned thirty. I'm not sure
what my age had to do with it, but that's when
it stopped. Your poor mother. This had to be
the most difficult decision of her life. She may
yet change her mind and come back for you.
I'll pray for her. And for your *onkel*, who needs
comfort, too."

Only God knew if Leah would be better
off with her mother or not. Either way, Joseph

was going to need Anne's support and the support of the entire community. He faced a difficult time and a hard choice. The person she needed to talk to was Naomi Beiler, the woman in charge of the local widows' group. Naomi would know what to do and how to do it.

Joseph stood on Anne's steps for a long time staring out at his yearling goats in the pasture across the fence. They moved slowly, grazing quietly, their white-and-brown coats contrasting sharply with the grassland. A few of the young ones frolicked briefly and a mock battle broke out between two young bucks. They butted heads a few times, but they soon stopped and went back to grazing. The sky overhead was clear, but Joseph's mind was in a fog. He couldn't make sense of what had happened. The letter sat like a stone in his pocket. He pulled it out and read it again, hoping for a different answer. It hadn't changed. It still said Fannie wasn't coming back for Leah.

He couldn't accept that.

Fannie would change her mind. She couldn't leave her babe without a thought, not the girl he knew. Not his sister. She would return. It was just a matter of time before she realized what a terrible mistake she'd made. He tucked the letter away again. What he had to do now was take care of Leah until then. He would find a way.

Anne's wheelbarrow full of pumpkins sat off to the side of the porch. He grasped the handles and began pushing it up her lane. He almost dumped it once, but managed to right it in time. Her front wheel was more than a little crooked. When he reached her produce stand, he marveled at the assortment of vegetables, gourds and pumpkins that she had for sale. The vegetables and gourds were displayed in small bins. The pumpkins were lined up along the roadside. Tucked among the produce were pots of mums in a rainbow of colors. She had a green thumb, it seemed. He was unloading the wheelbarrow when a silver car pulled up beside him.

The window rolled down, and the woman driver spoke. "How much are the white pumpkins?"

He wanted to ignore her, but it wouldn't be right to offend one of Anne's customers. He looked around for a sign or price list but didn't see one. Finally, he shrugged. "I don't know.

I'm just delivering these. The woman who runs the place will be here shortly."

"I can't wait. What if I gave you twenty dollars for three of them? Would that be enough?"

If the woman drove away, Anne wouldn't get anything. Hoping he was making the right decision, he nodded. "I reckon it would."

"That's wonderful. I'll take the three large ones in your wheelbarrow." The trunk of her car lifted. She got out and offered him the bill. Joseph pocketed the money, loaded her pumpkins and then walked away quickly before he had to deal with anyone else.

His milking goats were lined up along the fence watching for him and bleating. They knew something was up. He was never this late with the milking. He waded through them and opened the gate that led to the milking parlor. The first dozen goats hurried through, and he shut the gate after them, stopping the rest. He could milk only twelve at a time. The others would have to wait their turn.

Inside the barn, the animals went up the waist-high ramp and followed each other to their places. He latched the stanchions around each of them and put their feed in the trays in front of them. When they were happily munching, he jumped down off the platform and moved to clean and dry the udder of each doe and attach the suction nozzles. As he did so, he examined each animal, looking for signs of injury or illness. When he was sure they were all sound, he turned on the machine and began the milking process. The milk flowed from the animals through clear plastic hoses to a collection tank that would keep the fresh milk refrigerated until a truck arrived and collected it three times a week. Joining a co-op of goat dairy farmers had allowed him to increase the size of his herd and have a steady market for his milk. He was almost at the point that he could afford to expand the herd again, but one man could only do so much.

Joseph went through his chores without really thinking about them. His mind was still focused on Fannie. How could she have left her baby? Why had she done it? Was a child that much of a hindrance to the career she wanted, or was there another reason she wanted him to keep Leah?

I'm desperate, Joe. She will be safe with you. I won't worry about her for a single minute. Please. I know this sounds crazy, but it's what's best for her.

What did his sister's words mean? Were they simply part of the lie she had concocted, or had she meant them? Shaking his head, he had to admit that his sister had become a stranger. He no longer knew what to believe.

Try as he might, he didn't see a way he could care for Leah alone. Not while she was so little. He was out of the house from sunup to sunset most days. Even with electric milking machines, milking eighty goats twice a day took hours. Besides his goats, he had a small farm to run. Growing his own feed reduced his milk production costs and made sure his animals received the best nutrition possible. With winter approaching, he wouldn't need to spend time in the fields, but this was when he caught up on equipment repairs and got ready for the spring kidding season. What would he do with the baby when he was out in the pastures all day and all night when the does were birthing? He couldn't be in two places at once. It would be different if he had a full-time helper. Or a wife.

He glanced out the barn window toward Anne's house. She said she would help him. Had she meant only today, or would she be willing to do more? He wouldn't know unless he asked, but he wasn't sure he should.

After finishing the milking, he returned to Anne's house. He pulled the twenty-dollar bill from his pocket. "I sold three of your white pumpkins to a woman when I took your wheelbarrow up there. I didn't know how much they were. When she offered this, I took it because she couldn't wait."

"That's fine. A little more than I would have asked, but I'm not complaining. *Danki.*"

He looked around the room. "Where is Leah?"

"Sleeping. I made a bed for her in the other room. I'll show you." She led the way to her office, where she had lined a large plastic laundry hamper with a quilt. Leah lay on her back making tiny sucking motions with her mouth. A trickle of drool glistened on her chin.

Joseph squatted on his heels beside the basket. He couldn't believe the difference between the screaming child he had shoved at Anne and this little dear. "She liked the milk?"

Anne smiled. "She loved it. I mixed it half and half with the electrolyte water just so it wasn't such a drastic change for her. Sometimes switching to a new formula can upset a baby's tummy unless you do it gradually.

She hasn't spit up or fussed since she finished her bottle."

He breathed a quick prayer of thanks that Leah wasn't screaming or hurting. He was more grateful than ever for Anne's knowledge and skill. "You have worked a wonder here."

"I'm glad she tolerated the goat's milk. I had no idea what to try next if she didn't. We would have had to take her to see a doctor."

Now was the time to see how much Anne was willing to do for Leah. Rising to his feet, Joseph hooked his thumbs under his suspenders and took a deep breath. "I have a proposal for you, Anne Stoltzfus."

Chapter Five

"I'm listening," Anne responded, waiting for Joseph to explain his odd statement.

A proposal. What did that mean? Was he going to ask her to take Leah again? Anne hardened her resolve. As much as she liked the babe, she couldn't be Leah's mother. What if something happened to her? The thought scared Anne to death.

Joseph shifted uneasily from one foot to the other. "I will help you get your fields harvested and fix what needs fixing around the farm in exchange for your help with Leah."

She folded her arms. "Exactly what kind of help?"

"Like a mother would do."

"I've already said I won't keep her."

"*Nay*, you mistake my meaning. Like a *kindt*

heedah. Feed her, bathe her, watch her while I'm working."

"You mean you will harvest my pumpkin crop if I will be Leah's nanny?"

"*Ja.* That is what I want. Would you accept such a bargain?"

"I don't know. I'll have to think it over."

It was a tempting proposal. Hauling her large pumpkins out of the field was backbreaking work. Some of them weighed over twenty pounds. As strong as Joseph was, he could do it easily. He could probably carry one under each arm and one in his teeth and still push a loaded wheelbarrow. She had only another week to get them all picked unless an early freeze hit, then she wouldn't have anything to harvest. His help would be a blessing.

But taking care of an infant? What would she be getting herself into? She had a produce business to run. She had mothers coming for prenatal and postnatal appointments. There was no telling when an expectant father would show up wanting her to come deliver a baby. She had three mothers due before Thanksgiving. What would she do with Leah then? Run her back to Joseph's home? Amish women didn't call for the midwife until they were ready to give birth. She wouldn't have time to waste.

Still, the idea of Joseph raising Leah alone was as hard to imagine as her raising his goats. If she agreed to his proposal, she would be able to keep an eye on the baby, make sure she was thriving. The big question was, could she do it without becoming too attached to Leah?

The memory of losing her baby lingered in the back of her mind. Loving a child meant risking heartbreak. She shook her head.

Joseph sighed deeply. "You don't want the job. I understand. May I take your laundry basket with me until I can get a crib for her?"

"What has she been sleeping in?"

"A cardboard box that I lined with a blanket."

"Of course you can use my basket. I'm sure the church will provide the things you need when they learn of your situation."

He picked up the hamper. "I can make do without their help. I will manage until Fannie comes back."

Anne frowned and tipped her head slightly. "I thought the letter said she wasn't coming back."

His face turned stoic. "She will. She'll see

what a mistake she has made and she'll be back. I know my sister."

Anne held her tongue. She wasn't so sure. She fetched a half-dozen bottles of milk she had made from the refrigerator. "These pink bottles are half milk and half my fancy water. The rest are plain goat's milk formula. If she keeps the first ones down, give her full-strength milk tonight."

"Will you write down the recipe for me if she does well on this?"

Anne's conscience pricked her. She wasn't doing enough to help him. She could tell by the look on his face that he was unsure of himself. It had to be confusing and frightening for a bachelor to suddenly find he was in charge of a baby. "I'll make all the formula for you if you bring me fresh milk every other day."

"*Danki.* I'm not much of a hand at cooking."

"Why does that not surprise me?"

A grin twitched at the corner of his mouth. "I appreciate all the help you've given me."

"You're *willkomm.*"

He walked out with Leah in the basket. Anne closed the door behind him, determined not to feel that she'd made a mistake. She couldn't accept his offer of a job. She delivered babies.

She didn't raise them. What she did raise was produce. And right now her stand was unattended.

While most people knew they could leave their money in her tin can and take the pumpkins or the vegetables that they wanted, some *Englischers* would simply drive by if no one was minding the stand. She needed to get up to the road. The last two weeks of October were her biggest sale days. Today, Saturday, would be especially busy.

She grabbed a sweater from the hook beside the door and walked out into the chilly morning. The smell of autumn was in the air as the wind blew fallen leaves helter-skelter down the lane in front of her. The good Lord had blessed her with a bountiful crop and kept the heavy frost at bay. Only He knew how much longer the good weather would last.

Her pumpkins were larger than usual this year and thick under the still-green leaves in the field, but a hard frost would put an end to all of them. She said a quick prayer for continued favorable weather and walked quickly toward the small open-fronted shack she had built at the edge of her property.

If her land had fronted a busy highway, she

would have seen more business, but the village of Honeysuckle was small and off the main state roads, so traffic was generally light. Her idea to post a sign out by the highway was paying off, though. She'd had twice as many customers this fall as last. Only Joseph had complained about the increase in cars on the road.

A horse and gray buggy sat parked beside her stand when she reached it. Anne immediately recognized the animal and looked for the owner. Dinah Plank was inside the shack inspecting some of Anne's white pumpkins displayed in a wooden crate. Anne called to her, "Morning, Dinah."

"Wee gayt's," Dinah answered with a wave. "A good day to you, too. I thought you would be in town at the farmers' market, selling your produce there."

"I took a load of vegetable and pumpkins in yesterday and Harvey Zook's boy is selling them for me. I thought it might be better to be open at both places today."

"Goot thinking."

"Can I help you find something?" Anne smiled at her friend. Barely five feet tall, the cheerful plump widow was an energetic gray-haired woman. Dinah lived in Honeysuckle above the Beachy Craft Shop, where she worked for Anne's friend Ellen Beachy. Soon to be Ellen Shetler. The wedding was planned for the first Thursday in November.

Dinah picked up a creamy white pumpkin and thumped it. "I wanted to make a few pies for Ellen's wedding. There's nothing like the taste of a warm pumpkin pie fresh out of the oven piled high with whipped cream. I get hungry just thinking about it."

"I agree. You will want some of my heirloom cooking pumpkins for that. They make the best pies." Anne gestured toward a smaller crate inside her stand.

"What about these white pumpkins?"

"I've tried them and they are okay, but I don't think they have as much flavor."

"I'll be sure and tell my friends as much. Naomi wanted to try some whites."

Naomi Beiler, the widow of their church's former bishop, was the unofficial leader of the local widows' group. The group planned benefit suppers and the like for people in need within their Amish community. They had recently held a haystack supper to raise funds for Mary and David Blauch after their son was born prematurely. The baby had had to be hospitalized for several months and the couple faced a huge medical bill. The Amish didn't carry health insurance but depended on the rest of the community to aid them in times of need. If their local church wasn't able to cover the cost, a plea would go out to neighboring churches to help. The way everyone looked out for each other was one of the most comforting things about living in an Amish community.

Anne thought about Joseph and Leah. Joseph didn't feel he needed outside help, but Anne knew he did. "Will you be seeing Naomi this morning?"

On most Saturdays, Dinah went early to the farmers' market in town, where she met friends from her widows' club for breakfast. "I think so. Why?" Dinah cocked her head to the side.

"I have a small project I'd like help with. Joseph Lapp's sister recently paid him a visit and left her infant daughter with him."

"What?" Dinah's eyes widened behind her glasses and her mouth dropped open. "He's a bachelor."

"Exactly. He has nothing for the child. No

crib, no bottles, only a few things he borrowed from me."

"What is his sister thinking? How long is he going to have the child?"

"I wish I knew. She may not be back."

"How sad. Fannie has been out in the *Englisch* world a long time. It must be three years now. You never met her, did you?"

Anne shook her head. "She left before I moved here. Joseph has lived alone for as long as I've known him."

"I'm sure he isn't an easy neighbor to get along with. He's not a friendly fellow."

"We'd get along better if he kept his fences fixed. He came over three weeks ago to tell me my produce stand was bringing too many cars down the road."

"I can see why that would bother him. His parents and the girl he planned to marry were all killed when a truck struck their buggy right at the end of his lane. Joseph and Fannie were thrown clear with barely a scratch. It was very sad."

Anne's heart contracted in sympathy. "I didn't know."

"It was *Gottes* will."

All things were the will of God, but knowing that didn't dull the pain of losing a loved one. Anne tried to imagine Joseph as a brokenhearted young man. "Was she a local girl?"

"Her family lives near Bird-in-Hand. She was the eldest daughter. I'll speak to Naomi, but all we need to do is talk to a few of the mothers at church tomorrow and ask for donations of baby items. I know my daughters-in-law have clothing they can spare. How old is the child?"

"About four months."

"I can pick up some formula for her in town today and bring it by this evening."

"That won't be necessary. It appears that Leah has a milk allergy. We are giving her goat's milk."

Dinah chuckled. "Joseph should have plenty of that. How many goats does he have these days?"

"I have never tried to count. All I do is shoo them out of my garden."

"Looking at all these pumpkins, I'd say you've done a good job of keeping them away. I'll take six of your best cooking ones, and I'll share your concerns about Joseph's niece with my friends. I'm sure we can come up with the things he needs. Who is watching the child while he is out working with his goats and in the fields?"

"No one. He wanted to hire me as a nanny, but I said no."

"Why? I would think taking care of a baby would be your cup of tea."

Anne turned and began rearranging the gourds she had on display. "Of course I like babies, but...I don't know. I'm busy with the stand. Besides, I could get called out for a delivery at any time. It would be hard to have a baby underfoot."

"I see." Dinah didn't sound convinced. Anne glanced her way. The sharp-eyed little woman didn't look convinced, either.

Sighing heavily, Anne folded her arms and admitted the truth. "I'm afraid I would become too attached to her. She is an adorable *bubbel*. I may never have children of my own and caring for someone else's child every day would be a reminder of that."

"Sounds as if you are already attached to her."

"*Nay*, I'm simply worried Joseph won't be able to take care of her."

"Then you should find someone to be the

kindt heedah. You must know of several girls who would do well at that."

"I can't think of anyone offhand. Who could get along with Joseph? He is an odd fellow."

Dinah chuckled. "I'll check around and give him a few names tomorrow after the prayer service."

"That is a fine idea. I'll tell Joseph." It was a good solution. Leah needed someone to look after her and Joseph could easily find someone. It didn't have to be her. Then she could stop worrying about them both.

After a busy day at her produce stand, Anne made her way home. The western sky was ablaze with purple, pink and gold-tinged clouds fanned out along the horizon. The air had a decided nip in it as the day cooled. She hoped it wouldn't freeze tonight.

She pulled her sweater close and hurried up the steps, but she stopped on the porch and glanced toward Joseph's house before she went inside. She cocked her head in that direction, but she didn't hear any crying. How was Leah tolerating her goat's milk? The question had been at the forefront of Anne's mind all day.

"At least he didn't come running over. She must be doing alright."

Anne shook her head. Now she was talking to herself. It was not a good sign. If she was going to sleep a wink tonight, she would have to see for herself that the baby was doing better.

Crossing the strip of brown grass that bordered her flower garden, Anne paused at the gate between her place and Joseph's. Was there really a reason to go to his door? If he needed her, he would come and get her. He had already proven that. Anne bit the corner of her lip.

"Checking on them is the neighborly thing to do." As Anne battled her indecision, she saw a light come on in his barn. He was with his goats. Where was Leah?

Anne took a deep breath. She would just ask about the baby and leave. Before she could go any farther, the light went off. She waited a few moments. He appeared at the barn door with her laundry basket in his hands. It seemed Leah would learn about goats from the cradle.

He caught sight of Anne and stopped. After a brief pause, he headed toward her.

"How did she do?" Anne asked when he was close enough.

He stopped at the fence and rested the basket

on the top board. "She did fine. Slept most of the day. The rash is gone. *Danki*."

Anne peered in the basket. Leah lay with her eyes closed, but she was making tiny sucking motions with her lips and then smiling in her sleep. Anne's heart turned over. She touched the baby's soft hair. "She's dreaming about her bottle."

"You solved her problem. I'm grateful."

Anne drew her hand back and clenched her fingers together. "I saw Dinah Plank this morning. She thinks she can find a nanny for you. She said she would give you a few names tomorrow after church."

"I don't need anyone. Leah sleeps while I work."

"She won't sleep this much for long. Then what?"

He scowled and lifted the basket off the fence. "Then she will be awake while I work. We'll be fine until my sister returns. Do not concern yourself with us. *Guten nacht*," he said sharply and turned away.

Anne watched him walk off and wished she had another fresh tomato at hand. First he wanted her help and now he didn't. He was the most irritating man she'd ever met.

Chapter Six

Anne drew several stern looks from Naomi Beiler during the three-hour-long church service on Sunday morning. She tried to concentrate on the hymns sung, on her prayers and on the preaching, but she couldn't. Joseph wasn't among the worshippers.

Where was he? What was wrong? Was Leah okay?

Anne glanced over again, covertly checking the rows of men seated on the backless benches across the aisle. Joseph's size made him a hard man to miss. Although there were close to fifty men and boys all dressed in dark coats and pants with their heads bowed, she knew she could pick him out easily. He simply wasn't there.

Her friend Ellen elbowed her and Anne

straightened. Naomi was looking her way again. Her stern look had changed to a definite scowl. Naomi was the unofficial monitor of proper behavior among the church members, particularly the young men and women.

Fastening her gaze on the large black hymnal in her hands, Anne started to join the singing only to realize she was on the wrong page. Blushing bright red at her blunder, she turned the page and joined in on the correct verse in a subdued tone. When the service was ended, she closed her book thankfully.

"What is wrong with you today?" Ellen leaned toward Anne as they filed out of the Hochstetler's barn. Each Amish family in the congregation took turns hosting the prayer meetings that were held every other Sunday in their home, workshop or barn, depending on where there was adequate room to seat the congregation on the wooden benches that were brought in for the day. This Sunday was the Hochstetler's turn. The congregation had outgrown the family's small house, but the wide hayloft of the barn had more than enough room. The meal that would be served afterward would still take place in the house, although the members would have to eat in shifts.

"Nothing is wrong with me." Anne stood on tiptoe to see over the women grouped together beyond the doorway. Maybe Joseph had remained outside with Leah rather than risk her disturbing the worshippers.

"I'm the one who should be nervous, but you are like a mouse on the kitchen counter watching for the cat."

Anne relaxed at Ellen's teasing and put her concerns aside. "Are you nervous? The wedding date is almost here."

"Only a little over a week away. We wanted to be the first wedding in the area, but now I wish we had planned it for later. There is so much to do."

"You have many friends who will lend a hand. It will all get done."

Smiling sheepishly, Ellen nodded. "You're right."

Anne looked over the worshippers again as the men came out of the barn carrying some of the benches that would be stacked and turned into seating and tables for the meal. "I was expecting to see Joseph Lapp today. He's not here."

"Maybe he has gone to visit someone."

"Maybe so. I saw his horse and buggy

hitched and waiting in front of his house when I left home this morning. I thought he was coming here." She had almost stopped to inquire about Leah, but she thought Joseph wouldn't appreciate her concern. He hadn't last evening.

Ellen touched Anne's arm. "I see *mudder* looking for me. We'll visit later." She left without waiting for Anne's reply.

Anne spied Lizzie Fisher beckoning to her and walked her way. The young widow of Abraham Fisher had recently suffered a miscarriage only weeks after her husband's death. Anne knew the pain of losing the baby would lessen in time, but the memory of her lost child would never go away. Happily, God had placed a new joy in Lizzie's life. She had fallen in love. The young man was her deceased husband's brother, Zachariah Fisher. They planned to marry next month, too. November was the time for weddings in Amish country and the announcements for several couples had been made in church that day. "Hello, Lizzie. How are you doing?"

"I'm doing well. I just wanted you to know that I took your advice about doing something in memory of my baby. Zach and I chose to plant a dogwood tree beside the house. He has fond memories of playing beneath one when he and Abraham were small. It will be a special place to both of us."

"I'm glad. I hope it brings you comfort."

"It already has. Dinah Plank mentioned that Joseph Lapp was looking for a girl to baby-sit his niece. I didn't even know he had a sister, let alone a niece. My oldest stepdaughter, Mary Ruth, is interested, but I wanted to ask if you think she would be right for the job before Zack approached Joseph with the offer. I know he hasn't been the best neighbor to you. I've seen his goats in your garden."

Anne understood Lizzie's concern. "Joseph is not the easiest fellow to get along with. I think an older woman would be better. I'd hate to have him hurt Mary Ruth's feelings with his gruff ways."

"Then I'm sure glad I asked. She can look for a job that will suit her better. *Danki.*"

After visiting for a few more minutes, Lizzie left to gather up her stepchildren and take them in to eat. Normally, Anne would have joined the others in a light lunch and then an afternoon spent visiting and watching the children at play. Today she couldn't get her mind off

Joseph and Leah. She had to find out why Joseph hadn't been in church.

She found Dinah and explained why she was leaving early. Dinah sent one of her sons to get Anne's horse and buggy, but before he returned, Naomi Beiler approached Anne, followed by a number of the women in the widows' group.

Naomi crossed her arms over her chest. "I understand Joseph Lapp is caring for his niece. Dinah tells me the child is only a few months old."

The woman had a voice that carried. A number of people nearby stopped talking and turned to listen. Anne suffered a niggling of regret at sharing Joseph's story so publicly, but their community was small and tight-knit. She took comfort in knowing his situation would become public knowledge sooner or later. "It's true. His *Englisch* sister left the babe with him. At first Fannie said she would be back for the child. But later she wrote to say she wanted him to raise Leah."

She saw and understood the disbelief on the faces around her.

"We will pray for Fannie," Lizzie said. "It must have been a heartbreaking decision to make. No mother could give up her child without enormous pain."

Anne knew exactly how true those words were.

Nodding to the women gathered near her, Naomi said, "Our group has decided to help."

"That's wonderful." Over the growing crowd, Anne saw Dinah's son had her horse hitched and waiting.

"As this won't require a fund-raising effort, I'm asking those families with infant items they can spare to bring them to the Beachy Craft Shop on Monday. I'll personally deliver them to Joseph as soon as we have some." Naomi frowned and looked about. "Where is he? I didn't see him in the service."

"The baby has been sickly. I'm on my way to check on them now." Anne hoped nothing was wrong.

Joanna Miller glanced at her husband, Wilmer. "We have a crib and dresser we can loan him and plenty of baby clothes that our youngest has outgrown. What do you think?"

Her husband nodded. "I reckon we could."

One by one, the families around Anne began offering to bring various items to the Beachy Craft Shop the following day. Anne's heart swelled with gratitude. Everyone was stepping up to help. It was always this way in their Amish community. People helped each other.

Anne smiled at her friends and neighbors. "*Danki*, I know Joseph will be grateful."

Naomi's eyes grew sad. "I often wish I had done more for Fannie when Joseph was raising her. She needed a mother's influence in her life, but he didn't see it that way and my husband was ill, so I wasn't able to help as I should have."

"We can only do so much," Anne said to comfort her.

"You are right. The past is the past. It can't be changed. Are you seeing my niece Rhonda Yoder this week? Her babe is due in another three weeks. She's nervous because it's her first child."

"I am seeing Rhonda on Friday. She's doing fine. I don't anticipate any problems, but I know how scary it can be for new moms."

"You have a way with them. Rhonda thinks the world of you and so does her husband," Naomi said.

Anne chuckled. "Rhonda will do fine. I'm more worried about Silas. He's the bundle of nerves in the family. I told him if he fainted,

I was going to tell everyone. I think he's as concerned about that as he is about dropping his new baby."

The group broke apart after that as the women went to get the midday meal ready. Anne thanked Dinah's son and climbed into her buggy. She wanted to rush home, but she didn't push Daisy to a faster pace. The mare was getting older and would soon need to be put out to pasture to enjoy her final years. She should have been retired last year, but Anne didn't have the money for a new horse. She would have to come up with it soon. A midwife without a fast horse was one who risked not catching a baby.

Twenty minutes later, she passed Joseph's lane and soon reached her own. Pulling to a stop in front of her barn, she saw that Joseph's horse and buggy was still hitched and waiting in front of his house. Something was definitely wrong.

Anne jumped down from the buggy. Leaving the mare hitched in case she was needed, Anne hurried through the gate and up to Joseph's porch. In spite of the fact that they were next-door neighbors, she had never set foot inside his home. Gathering her courage, she knocked. When he didn't answer, she opened the door and walked in. Joseph, like most Amish, didn't lock his doors.

The kitchen was empty. The sunny room had large windows that let in tons of morning light, but it was a mess. There were dirty dishes on the table and some piled in the sink, too. Several pots on the stove held the remnants of Joseph's recent meals. She called his name and heard a muffled sound from the doorway to her left. She peeked in the room.

Joseph was sprawled in an overstuffed chair. He was wearing his Sunday suit, but he had one shoe on and one shoe off, as if he hadn't quite finished dressing. He had a patch of tissue on his upper lip and one on his neck that bore small bloodstains. He must have cut himself shaving. His head lolled to one side, his hair was mussed and he was snoring softly. Leah lay snuggled tightly in the crook of his left arm. An empty baby bottle was sitting on a small table beside his chair.

Anne pressed a hand to her mouth as a tug of pity pulled at her heart. Joseph's exhaustion had clearly caught up with him. There were dark circles under his closed eyes that even his thick lashes couldn't obscure.

Leah stretched in her sleep and brought her tiny fist to her mouth. She nuzzled her fingers, frowned and screwed up her face, getting ready to cry. She was adorable, no two ways about it. Anyone who took care of her was sure to fall in love with the child. After all, Anne was halfway there already.

This wasn't her baby, but Leah was a baby in need. And Joseph was a man in need, too. It was wrong to pretend they should be someone else's problem. The good Lord had brought Joseph to her doorstep. Anne would not turn them away.

She stepped to Joseph's side and gently shook his shoulder as she called his name.

Joseph heard a voice coming from a long way away. It was a woman's voice. Fannie?

He tried to force his eyes open. They felt as if they were full of sand and he let them fall shut again. Just a few more minutes of sleep. That was all he needed. Just a few more minutes.

"Joseph, wake up."

"I'm up," he muttered. He wasn't, but sleep was fading.

"I'm going to take Leah from you. She's getting hungry."

Who was talking to him? Someone lifted the baby from his chest. He tried to hold on to her, but his arm was numb and it wouldn't move. He raised his head and blinked. Anne Stoltzfus stood in front of him with a silly grin on her face.

"What's so funny?"

"You are." She turned away.

Why was she laughing at him?

He let his head fall back. It didn't matter. He was too tired to care. Sleep tugged at his mind, but his numb arm was waking up. Pins and needles stabbed him. He rubbed his arm from elbow to wrist, trying to ease the discomfort. The sound of Leah fussing penetrated his mind. Where was she? He raised his head again.

Anne had her. Only she was in his kitchen.

His kitchen!

He sat bolt upright. "What are you doing here?"

She held a bottle of milk and tested its temperature by sprinkling it on her wrist. "When you didn't come to the prayer service, I got worried, so I came to check on you."

"I missed church?"

"*Ja*, you did." There was that silly smile again.

He drew his hands down his cheeks. "I must have fallen asleep. What time is it?"

"One o'clock."

He'd been asleep for almost four hours? It was the most rest he'd had since Leah arrived. Yawning, he rubbed his stiff neck. "I don't know why you thought you had to come barging into my home. We are fine."

"I can see that." She laughed, a sweet light sound that sent the blood rushing to his face.

Okay, he wasn't fine, but he would be. If only he could close his eyes for another half hour. Just a half hour. That was all he needed.

Anne came to stand in the doorway. Leah was sucking contentedly on the bottle she held. "Has she been fussing again? Is that why you aren't getting any sleep?"

"She wants to eat every two hours."

Anne nodded. "She's making up for lost time. You can finish your nap. Leah will be at my place when you get up."

"Okay. Wait. What?"

"I'm taking her for the rest of the afternoon and you're welcome."

"*Nay,* this isn't right. She's my responsibility."

"Don't be stubborn and prideful, Joseph. Leah is going to spend the day with me and when you come to pick her up, we'll talk about my salary."

"What salary?" He couldn't keep up with her. His mind was a complete fog.

"The one you will pay me to be Leah's nanny."

"I thought you didn't want to do that."

"I've changed my mind. I'll see you later. Have a nice rest. I suggest you lie down on the sofa. That way, your neck won't be so stiff."

He opened his mouth to reply. There was some argument he needed to make, but he couldn't summon the wits to figure out what it was. He heard the door close and silence filled the house. Blessed silence.

Leah was being looked after. Anne could take care of her better than he could.

Anne with the sweet laugh and the funny smile who hated his goats and threw tomatoes at him.

He'd go and get Leah in a minute. It was his last thought as he dropped off to sleep again. Oddly, he dreamed about Anne walking among his herd with a little girl at her side.

They were both laughing at the antics of the baby goats leaping around them. He smiled in his sleep.

Chapter Seven

It was barely an hour later when Anne looked up to see Joseph standing in her doorway. He wore a sheepish expression, but he looked as if he'd finally gotten enough rest.

"I've come for Leah," he said quietly.

"She's sleeping at the moment. I was about to have some pumpkin soup. I didn't stay for the meal after church. Would you like some? It's a new recipe, so I'm not sure how good it will be." Anne stirred the bubbling contents of her pot, tasted it one last time and nodded in satisfaction. It was okay, but not as good as her mother used to make.

"I reckon I could eat a bite if it's not too much trouble." He continued to stand by the door.

"*Wunderbar*. Have a seat." She gestured toward her small table.

He was still wearing his Sunday best. Anne realized she'd never noticed what a handsome fellow he was until now. Normally, they were having a disagreement over the fence or she was throwing tomatoes at him. She blushed at the thought.

"First I want to apologize." He shifted from one foot to the other.

"For what?"

"For being asleep in the middle of the day when you came to my house. I'm not a lazy person."

"Don't apologize for falling asleep with a babe in your arms. You aren't the first person to do that and you won't be the last. I tell all my new mothers to sleep when the baby sleeps. If mothers try to get their housework done when the babe is asleep, they wear themselves out in no time. Babies take a lot of work. That's why mothers need helpers. It's tough to get up and feed a child every two to three hours night and day for weeks on end."

"I've only been doing it a week." He sat down at the table.

"She seems to be tolerating the goat's milk well. She'll start sleeping for longer periods now."

"That's good to know. Did you say you were willing to be her nanny or did I dream that?"

Anne poured the hot soup into two bowls and carried them to the table. "I said I would."

"What made you change your mind?"

"I saw how exhausted you were and I realized I was being selfish not to help." She would simply have to keep in mind that Leah wasn't her baby. Anne would take care of her, but she wouldn't fall in love with her any more than she fell in love with the babies she delivered. Caring for mothers and babies was the calling God had chosen for her. She would do her best to honor that gift. Anne took her place at the table. It was small, and sitting across from Joseph had an intimate feel.

"Danki." Joseph bowed his head for silent grace. Anne did the same.

When he was finished, he picked up a spoon and took a sip of the soup. "Not bad. It could use a little more ginger."

She took a sip. As much as she hated to admit it, he was right. "I'll increase it to a half teaspoon next time."

He blew on the next spoonful. "My mother used to make pumpkin soup in the fall. I've tried to duplicate her recipe, but I've never managed to make a batch as good as hers."

"That is exactly what I was thinking when I made this today. Is it that our mothers were better cooks, or is it that we remember things tasting better because they are no longer with us?"

"A bit of both, I'm sure."

She thought of the pile of dishes in his kitchen. "Do you find it hard to cook for just yourself?"

"I don't cook anything fancy. Mostly, I warm up things from cans."

That made sense. She tended to do the same thing. Sometimes she ate standing at the sink because sitting alone at the table was...lonely. It had been ages since she'd shared her table with a man. Her brother lived in the next county and rarely visited. Occasionally, the bishop and his wife would stop in. Mostly, she ate alone.

"I do make my own chèvre cheeses," he said between spoonfuls.

Anne looked at him in surprise. "You make goat cheese? What kinds?"

"Soft cheeses mostly. They're easy to make and you can flavor them any way you like.

Garlic, chives, spices, even chopped walnuts and dried cranberries. It's great on toast."

"I'd love to try some."

It was his turn to look surprised. "You would?"

"If I show you how to make Leah's formula, can you show me how to make goat cheese?"

Anne was delighted to see a true smile spread across his face. "If you have cheese-cloth and lemon juice or vinegar, I'll show you how after I milk this evening."

"That would be perfect. I can make up a big batch of formula for Leah then, too."

"She sure likes that stuff. I'm glad you thought to try it. It was right smart of you."

"It was really more a process of elimination, but *danki*." Pleased with his compliment, Anne continued to eat her soup and the conversation ended. They ate in companionable silence until he sopped the last bit from his bowl with a piece of bread and popped it in his mouth.

"Would you like some apple pie for dessert?" Anne had intended to sell it at her stand tomorrow, but Joseph still looked hungry.

"I won't say no to apple pie. It's my favorite."

Anne rose to fetch the pie from the pie safe. "My favorite is strawberry-rhubarb. I have plans to start a large rhubarb patch in the spring."

"Rhubarb leaves are poisonous to goats."

"I didn't know that. I knew they were poisonous to dogs." In that case, she might start her patch by his rickety fence. Maybe that would get him to mend it once and for all.

"Where were you thinking of putting it?"

"Just south of my barn. If it makes them sick, won't they avoid it?"

"Not the young ones. If you plan on planting rhubarb there, I'll for sure have to put up new fencing."

Anne hid a smile as she sliced her pie. How easy was that? She sensed it was as close to an apology as he was willing to make, but it signaled the beginning of a truce between them. She slipped two slices of pie on white plates and carried them to the table.

He accepted the dish from her. "*Danki.* What are your plans for your pumpkin fields when the harvest is done?"

"I'll rake the dried foliage and burn it and then I'll plant corn there next year." She took a bite of her pie. The tart sweetness of the apples and cinnamon in her flaky crust was a perfect ending to the meal.

"I thought your pumpkins were your best-selling items."

"They are, but you can't plant pumpkins in the same field two years in a row. It's best to wait three years."

"Why?"

"Pumpkins produce fusarium fungus in the soil. It causes the fruit to rot if you plant in the same ground too soon. The fungus dies away after two or three years."

"Rather than raking it and burning it, how would you feel about letting my goats graze it?"

She couldn't help needling him a little. "I guess we already know they like pumpkin vines and the leaves don't make them sick."

"Goats like to explore and they often find ways out of their enclosures."

"I've noticed, and they normally find their way through your rickety fence into my garden."

He scowled. "Are you a woman who forever harps on old injuries?"

Okay, maybe not a truce. She glared at him. "Are you a man who won't admit it when he's in the wrong?"

His scowl deepened but he didn't say anything. The sound of Leah crying in the other room broke their staring contest. Anne pushed away from the table. "I'll get her."

Joseph stood, too. "I'll warm her bottle."

"It's in the refrigerator."

"I figured it would be."

Anne rolled her eyes but didn't reply. At least he was being helpful even if he wasn't going to admit his fences were in poor repair.

After changing the baby and soothing her, Anne carried Leah into the kitchen. Joseph stood at her stove with a bottle of formula warming in a pan. When he saw her, he picked up the bottle and tested the milk by sprinkling some on his wrist. "It's still too cold."

Sitting in her chair, Anne noticed his half-eaten dessert. "You didn't finish your pie."

"I will. It's too good to waste. I wanted to get Leah's bottle ready first." He came back to the table and sat down across from her. He picked up his fork and took a bite.

"I'm glad you like it," Anne said. The atmosphere was strained. Leah seemed to notice and started fussing.

Joseph looked up from his plate. "Do you want me to hold her?"

"She's fine."

"She likes to be up on your shoulder."

Now he was going to tell her how to hold a baby! Why on earth had she said she would work for him? Wanting to prove to him that no matter how she held Leah, the child was still going to fuss until she got fed, Anne lifted the babe to her shoulder. To her surprise, Leah quieted immediately.

"I figured out that she likes to look around." Leah was holding her own head up. It bobbed slightly, but her eyes were wide and interested. "I think you're right," Anne admitted.

"That was hard to say, wasn't it?" He swallowed the last piece of his pie and returned to the stove.

Choosing to ignore his jab, Anne took the opportunity to finish her own pie. After testing the formula again, he brought the bottle to her. "Have you any chores that need doing?"

Only essential work was done on Sunday. Anything in her garden would have to wait until the next day. "If you could feed Daisy, I would appreciate it."

"Daisy?"

"My horse." Anne gave Leah the bottle. The baby grabbed it with both hands and began sucking vigorously.

"I can take care of your animal. I'll be back after the evening milking."

"All right. Leah and I will see you then."

He started out the door, but paused and looked over his shoulder. "The lunch was good. *Danki.*"

As a compliment, it wasn't much, but she accepted it at face value. She smiled brightly at him. "You're welcome, Joseph. I'm glad you enjoyed it."

Nodding to her, he left and closed the door behind him.

Anne grinned at Leah. "He's a hard man to like, but I think he's growing on me."

Anne Stoltzfus was an annoying woman.

Striding toward her barn, Joseph tried to get the picture of her smiling at him out of his mind. The sight of her pretty lips parted just so and the sparkle in her eyes sent an awareness shooting through his chest and made his heart beat harder. It was an uncomfortable sensation.

He wasn't a foolish youth. He'd had women smile at him before. Ellen Beachy, Elizabeth Fisher, Saloma Hochstetler, they were neighbors and single women. They smiled at him whenever they chanced to meet, but they didn't make his head swim like this. What was different about Anne?

He opened the barn door and stepped into the dark interior.

Maybe it wasn't Anne. Maybe he was coming down with something. He pressed the back of his hand to his forehead and was disappointed by the coolness of his skin. He wasn't sick. He couldn't blame it on a fever.

Offering her a job might have been a mistake. He found a pitchfork and began throwing hay to her elderly mare.

"*Nay*, Leah needs a *kindt heedah*." He couldn't do it alone. Not until Leah was older.

He stabbed the fork into the ground. What was he thinking? Fannie would return soon. She would be back for her child. He had to believe that.

Anne was the most logical choice for the job until then. She lived close by. She knew as much about babies as anyone. Anne with the pretty smile.

Stop thinking about her lips.

He lifted the fork and began pitching hay with a vengeance. He wasn't attracted to Anne. "I'm tired. That's all. I'm imagining things."

They had lived next door to one another for

three years and he'd never once had a romantic thought about her. Just the opposite, in fact. She was annoying and fussy. She hated his goats.

He couldn't like a woman who hated his goats.

After finishing with Anne's horse, he went home and cleaned his kitchen. A neat house was something he enjoyed. Everything had a place and he liked everything in its place. Since Leah's arrival, he hadn't found a moment to tidy up. Anne must think he was a slob. He'd have to have her over soon so that she could see he wasn't.

He shook his head. It didn't matter what Anne thought of him. Her job was to take care of Leah.

He took full advantage of the baby's absence and scrubbed the floor and counters, consoling himself with the thought that it was necessary work on a Sunday and all good housewives would agree.

Necessary to keep his mind off Anne and how she was getting along with the baby.

After he was done, he sat down to read from the Scriptures and from his well-worn copy of the *Martyrs Mirror*, a book that documented the stories and testimonies of Christian martyrs from the time of Christ to the 1600s. The trials endured by those people of faith gave him the courage to face the difficulties in his own life. Normally, he could immerse himself in the pages of the Holy Book or the *Martyrs Mirror* for several hours. But not today. He kept glancing at the mantel clock.

He milked at six o'clock in the evening, but by four thirty he gave up trying to read and went out to his milking shed. The goats filed into their stanchions, happy to see him even if he was early. By five thirty he had milked all eighty does, cleaned his equipment and made sure he had two gallons of fresh milk to take to Anne.

He retreated to his small office, a room partitioned in one corner of the barn where he kept his records, medical supplies and a propane-burning stove to warm the room in the winter. A brown leather office chair with the arms worn bare sat in front of a scarred metal desk and two filing cabinets. He made notations about the day's milk production and tallied his total gallons for the week. The herd's overall production was staying steady in spite of his neglect.

He left his office and carried the pails to the gate leading to Anne's property. As he opened it, he caught sight of Chester working his way under the wire near the back of Anne's barn. Leaving both pails by the fence, Joseph moved to stand over Chester until the animal had wiggled through. Taking the buck by the horn, he scolded him and led the culprit home. Instead of putting him back in his pen, Joseph shut the animal inside the barn in an empty stall.

"You stay in this time. I don't want that woman harping about your damages again. I've heard enough."

Chester bleated once, turned around twice and lay down in the straw. His attitude said he was home for the moment but not for good.

"Okay, I will put up new fencing but only to keep you alive. She's going to plant rhubarb."

Chester bleated again.

Joseph returned to his milk pails and carried them the rest of the way to Anne's house. He opened the door and paused at the sight of her rocking Leah in her arms and singing. She hadn't heard him enter. The soft smile on Anne's face, the light in her eyes, cut his breath short and made his heart flip over.

He couldn't like a woman who hated goats. He couldn't.

So what was this feeling?

Chapter Eight

Anne glanced up to see Joseph standing at the door with a steel pail in each hand. He had the oddest expression on his face. As if he'd never seen her before and didn't know who she was.

"You're back already?"

His expression quickly changed to his normal frown. "I finished early. What do you want me to do with this milk?"

"Set it on the table. Are you still willing to show me how to make cheese?" She wasn't sure what was wrong, but she sensed he was upset about something. Had she done something wrong or was he always this grumpy?

He took a deep breath and managed a half smile. "If you're willing to teach me how to make Leah's formula."

"Absolutely. Hold her while I get my pans ready."

After putting the milk on the table, he turned to her and she gingerly transferred the baby to his arms. Standing close to him brought a rush of heat to her face. Stepping back quickly, Anne regained her composure. She didn't normally react this way. She'd handed dozens of men their newborn babies. Why did being near Joseph fluster her? Perhaps it was because she felt sorry for him.

That had to be it. He was ill equipped to take care of the baby. His only sister had disappointed him again and was making his life difficult. If becoming Leah's father was the path God had chosen for Joseph, Anne would do all she could to help him.

"Shall we make cheese first, or shall we make formula?" she asked without looking at him.

He sat down in the rocker. It creaked under his weight but held. "Makes no difference to me. The cheese is probably simpler."

"How do I start?"

"You need four quarts of goat's milk and a good pinch of salt. I like to use minced or dried onions to flavor mine. Then you add one-third cup of distilled white vinegar or lemon juice. It doesn't matter which. I like using lemon juice."

"That's it?" Somehow she'd imagined it would be much more complex.

"I told you it was easy. Bring the milk to a slow boil at 180 to 185 degrees. Be careful not to scorch it. Add the dried onion and salt. Once the milk really starts bubbling, turn off the heat and pour in the vinegar. After that, you wait for the milk to curdle, then pour it through a colander lined with two layers of cheesecloth. Wrap the ends of the cheesecloth together and let it hang for an hour and a half or until all the whey drips off."

"What about saving the whey?"

"I close the ends of the cheesecloth with a rubber band and then slip a long-handled wooden spoon through it and suspend my cheese in a big jar. I keep the whey to make soup stock. Once the cheese is cool, you can add any spices that you like, shape the cheese into a ball or a log and refrigerate it. It will keep for a week."

"I'm anxious to try some." She set about heating the milk and before long she had her cheesecloth-and-curd bundle suspended and dripping into a widemouthed jar. By this time, Leah was sound asleep, so Joseph laid her in the laundry-basket crib and joined Anne by the stove.

Anne gave him an apologetic look. "I wish the formula making was as easy."

"I'm not afraid to learn something new. I will master it."

He had the right attitude. She laid a sheet of paper on the counter. "You have to heat the milk and add a number of ingredients such as cod liver oil, vitamins, blackstrap molasses, yeast and others. I've written down the recipe and the steps. I'll let you go ahead and make it while I watch. If you are confused or need help, I'm here."

It was dark outside and for the next hour, they worked by lantern light in Anne's kitchen to finish the project. Even she had to admit that he mastered the process quickly. After cleaning and boiling the baby bottles and nipples, they filled a dozen with eight ounces of liquid each. Joseph glanced at the clock. "It's getting late."

"I know it is time-consuming, but you can

make enough to last her three days in a single batch."

"I meant I should be getting home. It isn't proper for me to be in your house this late."

It wasn't likely that anyone would see them together, but he was right. She appreciated his thoughtfulness. "I will keep Leah with me tonight."

"Are you sure?"

"You could use an uninterrupted night's sleep."

"What if you have to go out on a call?"

"Leah can go with me."

Joseph shook his head as a chill raced down his spine. "I don't like the idea of her traveling in a buggy at night. The *Englisch* drive too fast. It's dangerous."

"Were your parents killed at night?"

So she knew about that. It shouldn't have surprised him. It had happened before she moved in, but it was common knowledge. "*Ja*, it was dark. The truck didn't see us until it was too late."

"I am sorry for your loss."

"It was a long time ago. It was *Gottes* will."

She laid a hand on his arm. "Knowing that

doesn't ease the pain of losing someone you love."

Joseph felt the warmth of her touch even through the material of his sleeve. The kindness and understanding in her eyes brought a lump to his throat. "It should help. We must believe in *Gottes* plan."

"We do believe, but we must also grieve, for that is how He made us. There is no shame in our tears."

"You have lost someone?"

He sensed her hesitation. Finally, she said, "My mother and my father have been called home, too. They lived long and devout lives and they were ready to face *Gott.*"

He didn't know if his parents and Beth had been ready or not. He hoped they had been. He'd simply frozen when the headlights blinded him. He hadn't thought about God. His only thought had been that he didn't want to die. He swallowed hard to clear his throat. "I was driving that night."

"It would not have mattered, Joseph. It wasn't your time."

It should have been.

The moment the thought crossed his mind,

he pushed it aside. God was not finished with him. He still had an unknown purpose to fulfill. Maybe it was to raise Leah. He hoped not. Leah needed her mother. He was a poor substitute.

"I must go. *Guten nacht*, Anne Stoltzfus. I will move more pumpkins to your stand for you in the morning if you'll show me which ones you want." In spite of his discomfort at being near her, he didn't want to leave. She had a peaceful quality that eased the ache in his soul.

Chuckling, she said, "Just pick the orange ones, Joseph. As many as you can find."

She was laughing at him again. He hardened his heart, determined not to like her.

He was meant to be alone. He had accepted that long ago in the months after Fannie left the first time. To care for someone was to invite heartache. It was better to keep the world at bay. Especially a pretty *maidel* with a kind heart and a smile that lit up her eyes like stars twinkling in the night sky.

Angered at the direction of his thoughts, he turned and left. Later that night, as he tried to make his tired mind stop spinning, he found himself remembering each moment of their evening together. Sighing, he punched his pillow into a more comfortable position and turned over. The moonlight bathed his room in a pale glow. The box he had used as a bed for Leah sat empty. He missed her presence. Was she keeping Anne up?

He rose and stepped to the window that overlooked her home a few hundred yards to the north. It was dark. Leah must be sleeping and he should be, too.

He was about to return to bed when he saw a light come on in Anne's upstairs window. After a few moments, the lantern light moved down to the kitchen. He watched until the first-floor light went out and the upstairs window grew bright again.

It was easy to imagine Anne holding Leah and singing to her in a low sweet voice as the baby gobbled up her nighttime bottle. Leah would be making faces and Anne would be grinning at her. Anne had the patience he lacked. She was good with the child.

Why hadn't she married? Why wasn't she a wife and a mother? Was it because of her job? Most Amish women stopped working outside the home once they married, but the local midwife was often the exception to the rule. They were nearly always married women or widows.

He'd lived next to Anne for three years and yet he knew next to nothing about her. Maybe it was time he put aside his need for privacy and got to know her better. She would be caring for Leah until Fannie came back. In the dead of night, he couldn't push aside the fear he kept at bay during daylight. The fear that Fannie wouldn't return. Ever.

He didn't want to believe the words she'd written. He needed to believe she would have a change of heart. He'd never give up on her. Not even now. As he did every night, he prayed for her. Bowing his head, he asked God to send her the comfort she needed. It was with a heavy heart that he returned to his bed, but he had the consolation of knowing Leah was being cared for by someone with a kind, gentle nature.

The next morning, he finished his milking early and headed to Anne's place. He opened the front door and was greeted by the smell of cinnamon toast and frying bacon. Leah lay on a bright quilt in the center of the kitchen floor. Holding herself up on her elbows, she kicked her feet as she tried to reach a pair of yellow plastic measuring cups in front of her. She was making little cooing sounds.

"You can wash up at this sink. Breakfast will be ready in about five minutes. Do you want coffee or orange juice or both?" Anne asked over her shoulder.

"I didn't expect you to feed me."

"There are a lot of pumpkins to move. You will need your strength. Besides, it doesn't take much more effort to make breakfast for two instead of one."

He washed his hands and then squatted on his heels beside Leah. He moved one of the measuring cups closer. She grasped it in her chubby fingers and pulled it to her mouth. "Just *coffe* for me. She seems happy this morning."

"*Ja*, she does. She only woke up once last night and she went right back to sleep after she ate."

Leah rolled onto her back and grinned at him as she chewed on the handle of her prize. "Is that tasty?" he asked. The baby gurgled in reply and he smiled. "I think she is trying to talk to me."

"Babies this age like to interact with others."

"I thought they just ate, slept and needed their diapers changed."

"They do that, too. I have sweetened some of the cheese we made with honey and lemon peel. It tastes wonderful on warm toast." She carried a platter of bacon to the table.

"I told you it was good."

He took a seat and lifted Leah to his lap. She kicked in delight and cast her plastic cup aside. He retrieved it and gave it back to her. Grinning, she dropped it again. He picked it up. "You did that on purpose."

She gnawed on the lip for a second, then dropped it again and giggled. Anne sat down at the table. "You two seem to have discovered a new game."

"I can't believe the difference in her. She did nothing but whimper and cry and fuss for me."

"It wasn't you. She was hungry but in pain every time she ate. She was miserable. Hopefully, those days are behind her."

He settled Leah in his lap and folded her hands inside his as he said a silent blessing before eating. It was the way Amish parents taught their children to behave at the table. Although Leah was too young to understand, she would come to know that sitting quietly with her hands folded was expected of her. When he finished praying, he shifted her to the crook of his left arm. The baby discovered his suspenders and began trying to bring the stretchy material to her mouth.

"I can take her," Anne offered.

"*Nay*, she is fine where she is. What are your plans for today?" He enjoyed watching Leah struggle with the elastic material. An adorable frown formed on her face when it got away from her, but she grabbed it again.

Anne said, "The last week of October is my busiest time. I will sell the bulk of my pumpkins in the next few days, so I have to be at the stand as much as possible. I need you to bring all my pumpkins out of the field. I'll take Leah's laundry-hamper bed up to the shack and she can stay there with me as long as the weather stays decent."

"I heard it may rain tomorrow."

"I hope not. Bad weather means fewer shoppers. The leaves and vines are very prickly, so wear gloves when you go into the field. It will keep you from getting itchy."

"I appreciate the advice. Anything else I should know?"

"When you cut them off the vines, leave a stem about four to six inches long, but don't try to carry them by the stems. They'll break."

"Got it."

Leah gave up on his suspender and threw her cup on the floor again. Joseph sighed heavily as he picked it up. He hesitated but decided to give it to her. She grinned and cooed her delight. For such a smile, he could pick up her toy all day long.

Please, Lord, let her remain as happy and contented as she is at this moment.

After breakfast he helped Anne move the supplies she and Leah needed up to the small shack she had at the end of her lane. There were already two cars parked at the side of the road and a number of small children examining the pumpkins. He left Anne to deal with her customers and took her small wheelbarrow out into the pumpkin patch. She hadn't been kidding about the prickly vines and leaves. What she'd forgotten to mention was how easy it was to get tripped while trying to carry a ten-or fifteen-pound pumpkin out of the vines to the wheelbarrow. By his third foray into the field, he decided he would use his own pushcart the following day. It was larger and easier to move.

The next day went by much like the day before, although he fixed his own breakfast. He had agreed to work in her fields in exchange for her services as Leah's nanny. He hadn't agreed to be fed. He left Leah with Anne before sunup while he did his chores and then he returned to help her move more pumpkins and produce to her stand.

Anne cleaned and polished the orange fruit and arranged them according to size on several tables. Traffic was light but steady throughout the morning. With each large pumpkin Anne sold, she gave away a small one and a sheet of paper.

"What are you handing out?" he asked when her latest customer drove away.

"It's my recipe for homemade pumpkin pie and for roasted pumpkin seeds. I'm hoping folks will enjoy them and come back for more of my cooking pumpkins next year."

"That's a *goot* idea. A way to provide customers with more than they expected and a way to encourage repeat business. I'm impressed."

"Danki." She smiled her thanks at him and blushed sweetly.

A flutter of pleasure deep in his chest caught him by surprise. When had this foolishness overtaken him? He had been fetching toys to make Leah smile at him and now he was handing out compliments in order to make Anne smile, too.

He had to admit he was beginning to like Anne. There was something about her that made him want to please her. It was more than her care of Leah. It was the way she seemed to care about him, too. A smile spread over his face. He sensed a friendship growing between them and he liked the feeling.

A pair of buggies approached, so he wiped the grin off his face. Leah started to fuss as she woke up. He and Anne both dropped down to pick her up and bumped their heads together in the process.

He shot to his feet. Anne did, too, but she stepped on the hem of her long skirt and stumbled forward into him. He caught her in his arms. He steadied her until she regained her balance. She stepped back quickly, her face flushed a bright red. He apologized. "I'm so sorry."

Rubbing her forehead, she said, "It's okay. I'm not hurt. Much."

He caught a glimpse of Preacher David Hostetler and his sons scowling at him as they drove past. He chose to ignore them. "I've been accused of having a hard head."

Anne chuckled. "So have I, but I think you win. I'm going to get a bottle for Leah. You can hold her."

He picked the baby up. As Anne walked down the lane, his gaze followed her. There was a soft sway in her walk that he found attractive. There were a lot of things he was finding attractive about his neighbor. Why hadn't he noticed them before?

He bounced Leah in his arms, keeping her occupied by making faces at her until he saw Anne returning.

Before she reached him, a horse and wagon came down the road and drew to a stop in front of the stand. Naomi Beiler was driving, but two other women sat beside her. He recognized them as widows from his church group. Behind her came Simeon Shetler driving his two-wheeled cart loaded with boxes and baskets. Dinah Plank sat beside him. Simeon had lost a leg in an accident as a young man. Now a grandfather, he got along well on his crutches. He could often be seen driving his cart and palomino pony named Butterscotch, the only animal in the area more notorious for escaping his pen than Chester.

Naomi leaned toward Joseph. "Is that your

niece? What a pretty *bubbel*. Anne has told us all about your wayward sister and how she has burdened you with her child. You have our sympathy, brother."

Humiliation burned like acid in Joseph's belly. Gritting his teeth until the muscles in his jaw ached, he snatched the bottle from Anne's hand as he glared at her. "You didn't waste any time spreading gossip about me behind my back, did you?"

Chapter Nine

Anne saw the fury in Joseph's eyes, but underneath his anger, she saw his pain, too. She had hurt him. How could she fix this? "It wasn't like that, Joseph. I wasn't spreading gossip. These women have come to help."

"I told you I don't need anyone's help." He stomped away and Anne realized what a dreadful mistake she had made.

Naomi stepped down from her wagon. "Is everything all right? Have I said something that I shouldn't have?"

"*Nay*, this was my mistake. I didn't tell Joseph that you were coming. I meant to, but I just didn't expect you so soon. Joseph is embarrassed by his sister's behavior. I think he feels he is to blame for raising her poorly."

"We all feel shame when our children disappoint us. Even a child raised in a righteous household can stray. *Gott* granted every man and woman a free will, and so they must use it to find their way to Him or to reject Him. What do you want us to do with the things we have collected? Our community has been very generous."

"They always are. Let's take the things to Joseph's house. He will soon realize our intention is to help, not to criticize."

Anne walked to Simeon's cart. "Dinah, if you could stay here at the stand and take care of any customers, I'll show the others where to put things."

"Of course, dear." The widow smiled warmly at Simeon and got out of his cart.

Anne accepted his hand and took Dinah's place on the front seat. "One pretty gal after another riding in my cart today. I'm a blessed man."

Simeon was known as a bit of a flirt, but he was a kind man and he would never cross the lines of propriety. Like some others, Anne had begun to suspect Simeon and Dinah were becoming more than friends. It would be a good match for the widow and widower. After turning his pony around, Simeon led the small procession down Joseph's lane and stopped in front of his house.

Joseph and Leah were nowhere in sight. Anne helped everyone carry in the supplies and furniture. To her amazement, the inside of Joseph's home was spotless. All the dishes had been washed and put away. She could tell the kitchen counters and floor had been scrubbed. It was quite a change from the last time she had stepped inside his home.

She directed the women to put the crib and a small dresser in Joseph's living room. He could move it elsewhere if he didn't like the placement. The women folded and placed all the baby clothes and blankets in the dresser drawers and put clean sheets on the crib mattress. The basket of a dozen baby bottles and rubber nipples was left on the kitchen counter. A second basket, a woven Moses basket made to carry the baby around, held an assortment of infant toys. Rattles, colored stacking blocks and a teething ring were but a few of the items in it.

There were also a half-dozen boxes of infant rice cereal and baby food that Leah wouldn't need for a few more months, but when she did, Joseph would be well supplied. Looking over the generosity of the community moved Anne to add something of her own.

She went home and climbed up into her attic. She opened a chest there, withdrew a paper-wrapped parcel and returned to Joseph's place. After everyone filed out of the house, Anne pulled off the wrapper and laid her contribution, a beautifully stitched baby quilt, over the end of the oak crib. She gently smoothed the wrinkles from the material. As she did, her thoughts turned to her own baby. For a minute her regret and grief were so intense she almost broke down. Joseph had no idea how blessed he was to have Leah, but she did. Blowing out a deep breath, she straightened her shoulders and went outside.

She walked over to Naomi's wagon and spoke to the women seated there. "*Danki.* I'm sorry Joseph isn't here to thank you himself, but he will soon realize what a wonderful community he lives in. I hope your generosity opens his heart to the goodness that surrounds him."

Naomi nodded. "I will not let him struggle to raise this child alone as I did when Fannie was small."

"We will all do better," Simeon said as he

held out a hand to help Anne into his cart again. She climbed up. He turned the pony and sent the animal trotting up the lane. At her roadside stand, she thanked Dinah for taking care of her customers and waved as the group drove away.

The early part of the afternoon went by slowly. With only two customers in the next two hours, Anne was left with plenty of time to think about Joseph. She would find a way to apologize to him. She should have listened to that small voice of unease that tapped on her shoulder after the church service, but she hadn't. She hadn't felt that she was betraying his trust when she shared his story, but it was clear he felt she had gossiped behind his back. Had she lost his trust for good?

Would he let her continue to care for Leah? Or would he find someone else? Anne was distressed to realize just how much she would miss the baby if he decided to replace her with a different *kindt heedah*.

And that was exactly why she shouldn't have taken the job in the first place.

Maybe it would be for the best if he did find someone else. The longer she took care of Leah, the harder it would be to let someone else take over.

"Can you watch her while I milk?"

Anne spun around at the sound of Joseph's voice. She hadn't heard his approach. He wore a wary expression and held the baby in his arms. She was wide-awake but content to suck on her fingers.

"Of course I can. That was our agreement."

"Danki." He handed the baby to her.

Anne struggled to quell the rush of breathlessness being close to him inspired. He stepped back quickly and shoved his hands in the pockets of his dark jacket. He wouldn't look at her.

The easy camaraderie they had shared that morning was gone. Only an awkward silence remained.

"Joseph, I'm sorry. I didn't mean to embarrass you. I wanted to help you and Leah."

"You should have told me to expect them."

"Ja, I should have. I honestly intended to do so. I wasn't expecting them to show up this morning. Naomi can move mountains when she sets her mind on something. She feels very

badly that she wasn't around to help you with Fannie when she was young."

"We managed."

"I know you did, but you deserved more help than you were given. I know Bishop Beiler was ill then, but did he visit you?"

"I went to see him."

"What did he say?"

"The truth."

"I don't understand."

Joseph sighed deeply. "The driver that hit us claimed the accident was my fault. He said he wanted me to pay for the damage to his vehicle or his insurance company would take my father's farm. My farm. I didn't have that kind of money, but I agreed to pay him over time. I took a second job working for him to pay off the debt. It was hard to keep food on the table in those first months. I went to the bishop to ask if Fannie could be placed with another family until I got on my feet. Bishop Beiler told me raising Fannie was my duty. She was my responsibility and I wasn't to foster her off on someone else so that my life would be easier."

Anne flinched. It had been a harsh thing to

say to a grieving young man. "I'm sorry he misunderstood what you needed."

Joseph drew himself up straight. "I know my duty. I will care for Leah until her mother returns."

"And I have agreed to help you. That hasn't changed...unless you wish to fire me."

Watching the struggle going on behind his eyes was painful for Anne. It wasn't pride that kept him from seeking help. It was a misplaced belief that he needed to do it alone.

She wasn't going to let him. If he needed to believe she was helping only because of their business arrangement, so be it.

Gesturing to her display, she said, "I will need at least two dozen of the biggest pumpkins brought up here first thing in the morning. Do you think you could build a shelf to display them? Something at eye level for the children. The *Englisch* parents seem to want the *kinner* to pick out their own pumpkins. Do you have any ideas?"

He studied her for a moment, then pushed his hat back with one finger and surveyed what space she had. "If I brought up some straw bales, I could lay a couple of planks across them. That would put your pumpkins about waist high. Would that work?"

"That would be perfect. Finish the milking, Joseph, and I'll bring Leah to your house when I'm done here. Have you been inside the house since noon?"

The wary expression returned to his eyes. "*Nay*, I've not."

"The church ladies left some infant items for you to use. Just until Fannie returns. They'll be back to pick them up when you don't need them anymore. It's a loan, Joseph."

"I still wish you hadn't said anything."

She gave him an apologetic look. "I shouldn't have spoken without your permission. I'm sorry I upset you, but it was for Leah's sake."

His scowl remained, but he didn't comment. Could he forgive her interference? Anne gazed at the baby in her arms. "She deserves a better bed than my laundry basket, and now she has one."

"Until Fannie returns."

"Until her *mudder* returns," Anne agreed. She saw a car slowing down as it approached and knew she was about to have another customer.

Joseph pulled a bottle from his coat pocket

and held it out. "I thought she might get hungry again before my chores were done."

"*Danki.*" Anne's fingers brushed across his as she took the bottle.

Her soft touch sent a wave of warmth flooding through Joseph. As much as he wanted to stay angry with her, he couldn't. He knew she had Leah's best interests at heart. She didn't believe he could care for the baby alone and maybe she was right. Wasn't that what he feared? He'd certainly done a miserable job so far.

Maybe if she had been around when Fannie was small, things would have turned out differently for his sister. Fannie had needed someone like Anne. Someone to be a mother to her. Maybe he should have married for her sake.

He pushed the thought aside. He couldn't change the past.

When a car pulled to a stop beside them, he left Anne to speak with her customer and went to milk his goats for the second time that day. He'd spent very little time with his animals in the past few days and they gathered around him now when he entered the pen. Matilda rushed to his side and butted him gently in greeting. He paused to scratch behind her ear and murmur a few kind words. More of the young does came seeking attention, too.

He knew each one of them by name, who their dames were and who their grandmothers had been, and how much milk they produced each day. The goats had kept Fannie and him fed during the lean times after their parents and Beth were killed. Then the goats became his life after Fannie left. He'd lavished his affection on them because there'd been no one else to receive it. Until now. Now he had Leah. The thought made him as frightened as he had been when he realized he would have to raise Fannie. More so. A babe Leah's age required almost constant attention.

Matilda butted him again when he stopped petting her. He gave her a wry smile. "You are right to be jealous, but don't worry. Leah will soon be big enough to visit you and bring you apples and cereal when I'm not looking."

Just as Fannie had done. Did she miss them at all?

He couldn't imagine his life without the goats' playful, happy personalities greeting him each day. Their affection never wavered.

They might wander away, but they always came home.

In a nearby pen, the young rams started showing off, jumping on the large boulders he'd piled together for them to climb on and play around. He would sell them in the spring. Their mothers were among his best milk producers and that bloodline would command a good price from other goat dairymen looking to expand their herds. Joseph hated to sell any of his goats for meat, but sometimes he had to do so.

He spent an extra thirty minutes with his animals, checking for any injuries or illness he might have overlooked in the past hectic week. They were all healthy. Only Chester was sulking because he was still penned in the barn. He refused to greet Joseph until fresh hay appeared over the stall door. Where food was concerned, Chester had a forgiving nature and he sprang to his feet and rushed to be fed. Joseph scratched the old fellow behind his ears, too.

When he couldn't put it off any longer, Joseph walked up to the house. Anne was there ahead of him. She was holding Leah on her hip as she stirred something on the stove with her free hand.

"I had some leftover vegetable soup that I thought you might like for supper."

"You don't have to feed me. That wasn't part of our bargain."

"I know, but I hated to throw it out. Normally, I'd take it into the Beachy Craft Shop and store it in my freezer there, but I didn't feel like making a trip into town this late in the evening."

As excuses went, it was a little lame, but the delicious smell was enticing enough to keep him from complaining further. "I have electricity in my barn. If you ever want to move your freezer closer, you could put it out there."

"With the goats?" She wrinkled her nose.

"I have an office in there. The goats don't go in that part of the barn."

"I thank you for the offer. I'll consider it."

He noticed the basket on the counter beside her. "Is this what the church donated?"

"Some of it." She kept her eyes averted.

Her friendly smile was missing and he hated that. Shame kept him from apologizing, as he knew he should. Being the object of charity stung. It was vain pride and he knew it. He opened the lid of the basket. "I reckon I'd better see what they provided to this poor, needy man."

Pulling out the bottles, he counted them. Twelve. It would be easy to make enough formula to fill them and have them handy in the refrigerator. A second large box sitting beside the counter was full of disposable diapers and several packages of cloth ones, as well as baby wipes. A true blessing. He opened a third box and held up a package with the picture of a grinning baby on it. "What is this?"

"Rice cereal. She's too young for it yet. Most *mudders* start cereal when the babe is six or eight months old."

"And the baby food in jars?"

"Also when she is about six to eight months old. It varies. Always start with a single food in case she has a reaction to it."

"Do you think she'll have trouble with these since she can't tolerate cow's milk?"

"There isn't any way to know. She might outgrow her problem or she might not. There are some more items in your living room." Her tone was clipped, professional, as if she were talking to a stranger. She wasn't smiling. He missed her smile.

He entered the living room and saw a beautifully crafted sleigh-style baby crib against the wall by his sofa. A dresser of the same rich oak finish sat beside it. They had both been polished to a high sheen. A bumper pad and sheets in pale yellow completed the set. Over the end of the bed hung a small puffy crazy quilt with blocks and triangles in primary colors. He ran his fingers lightly over the padded fabric and marveled at the tiny neat stitches.

"There are some extra sheets and clothes for her in the dresser drawers," Anne said from behind him.

He swallowed against the lump in his throat. "This is more than I expected. It was a nice thing for folks to do. I'll take good care of it all."

"I know you will, Joseph," she said quietly.

He was afraid to meet her gaze. Afraid he wouldn't see her smile. He wanted to apologize for his harsh words earlier that afternoon, but something kept him silent. Anne didn't understand. Leah was his responsibility, not hers, not the church's, his.

Anne slipped past him and laid Leah in the crib. They stood side by side watching the

baby drift off to sleep. When Leah was settled, Anne said, "Good night, Joseph."

She left the house before he could think of
some way to stop her.

He ate his supper alone, already missing
Anne's presence. There was something special in the air when she was near. The autumn
evening was cooler without the warmth she
radiated.

Later that night, as he stood at his bedroom
window and watched the lights go out in her
home, he wondered what she thought of him.
Was she angry? She had the right to be. He'd
accused her of spreading gossip behind his
back. If only he could call back those words.

He didn't want his relationship with her to
return to the way it had been. Distant. Cool.

He didn't have many friends. He didn't want
to lose Anne's friendship. How could he earn
it back?

Chapter Ten

The following morning, Joseph found it was easier to care for Leah when he could safely leave her in the crib while he prepared his breakfast and got her morning bottle ready. She was delighted with the new toy he'd found for her, hard plastic keys that clacked when she shook them. They kept her occupied and quiet for the twenty minutes he needed.

After feeding her, he put her in the stroller on his front porch and pushed her to Anne's house. Dawn was just breaking. The eastern sky was streaked with bands of high pink clouds. The forecasted rain was holding off, but it was already cooler than the day before. Anne wasn't in the kitchen and there was no answer when he called up the stairs. Had she gone out to deliver a baby?

Stepping back on her front porch, he saw her mare in the corral, so he knew she hadn't driven anywhere. Maybe she was already up at her roadside stand. Or was she avoiding him?

He dismissed the thought. She might choose to dodge him, but not Leah. He knew she genuinely cared for the baby. Movement out in her garden caught his eye, and he saw she was loading her rickety wheelbarrow with dried stalks of corn. He walked in her direction, unsure of his reception. She wore a dark blue jacket over a dress of the same color and a black apron. The ribbons of her white prayer *kapp* were tied behind her neck.

"Good morning, Joseph and good morning to you, too, Leah," Anne called out when she caught sight of them. Her smile seemed a little forced, but he was relieved to see it, anyway.

"What are you doing with those?" he asked, gesturing to the corn.

She brushed her gloved hands together. "I'm making some decorative bundles to sell. A woman who came by late yesterday asked for some. I told her I would have them ready this morning and she promised to be back."

He shook his head. "Decorative bundles of

corn. It seems like a waste of good livestock feed to me."

"To me, as well, but who can fathom the ways of the *Englisch*?" She began pushing the wheelbarrow toward the house.

He fell into step beside her. The large wheels of Leah's stroller rolled easily over the dry ground. "I should be able to gather the rest of your pumpkins this morning."

"I'm thrilled with how many I have sold, but I need to sell many more. Thursday is the last day of the month and the last day I will be open this season. I'm not sorry to see the end of October, but November will be busy, too."

"With produce?"

"*Nay*, with weddings and babies. I have three mothers due next month. Speaking of babies, how did Leah do last night?"

"We had our best night yet. She woke once, at two in the morning, took her bottle and went right back to sleep. I think she likes her crib."

"That's good to hear." Anne cast him a covert glance, but he saw it.

"I like it, too. It makes it easier to change her and I don't have to worry about her turning the laundry hamper over and rolling out."

"Has she done that?"

"Once," he admitted. "She rolled to one side and it tipped." He didn't mention that he'd had her on the sofa at the time and had barely caught her before she'd tumbled off.

"Then the crib is safer. I didn't realize she could turn over that well."

"She's strong." He stopped by Anne's porch. "I'll take your corn to your stand and then I'll get the rest of your pumpkins."

"I'll take Leah to the stand with me later. I have a mother coming for a checkup soon. Has Leah eaten this morning?"

"*Ja*, she had her bottle. We'll need to make more formula this evening. She's going through it fast."

"I'm just happy we discovered what was wrong with her." Anne crouched down to wipe the drool from Leah's face with the corner of her apron.

It was past time for his apology. He crossed his arms over his chest. "You have done a lot for us."

"Only my Christian duty."

"And I have been remiss in mine. I was wrong to accuse you of gossip. I know you thought you were doing what was best for Leah."

Anne rose to her feet. Her cheeks grew

bright pink. "I'm glad you realize that. I wouldn't hurt you for the world, Joseph."

"I reckon I can be stubborn as my goats sometimes. I see that I should have asked the community for help instead of struggling on my own."

"You have given to others many times in the years that I've known you. When John Beachy had that fire, you came to help. When Mary and David Blauch needed money for their son's medical bills, you gave. There's no shame in accepting help in return. It is what binds us together, our faith and knowing our church and neighbors will rally around us in times of need. We all need help at some point. We all give help when we can."

When she put it that way, it felt less like charity. "You're right. I was wrong."

Her eyes widened as she slapped a hand to her cheek. "Did I hear you correctly?"

He struggled not to smile and lost the battle. "Gloat if you must. You'll not hear that from me often."

Chuckling, she tickled Leah under the chin. "There is hope for your *onkel* yet. It's a wise man who admits his faults."

"It's a wiser woman who does not point them out," he shot back.

Laughing, Anne pushed the child toward her house. She glanced over her shoulder and he saw the bright smile he had been missing. It blew away the chill of the autumn morning and brought warmth to his heart.

Joseph lingered a moment as Anne went inside. She was a wise and kind woman. Hardworking and devout in her faith, she would make a fine mother and wife for any man. Once again he thought it was a shame she had never married. Although he wondered why she remained single, he didn't question her. That was too personal a subject.

After taking her corn up to the road stand for her, he returned to milk his herd and finish his morning chores. He rushed through his milking and cleaning. As he fed the bucks, he saw one of the young ones had a foot caught in the fence. It took a while to free him. By then the milk tanker driver had arrived and Joseph helped him empty the holding tank.

With that done, he went out to Anne's field and got to work. A short time later, he saw a buggy drive up to her house. A woman with a couple of children went inside. That had to be one of her mothers. He wasn't able to tell who it was. He was too far away. When he had the wheelbarrow full, he pushed it up to the house. He wasn't sure where Anne wanted the pumpkins stacked, so he stepped into the house to speak with her.

A little girl about five years old was trying to open Anne's large black leather satchel. She jumped away from it when she heard him come in, clasping her hands behind her back.

"What are you doing?" he asked.

"Nothing."

"It looks to me like you were getting into something that didn't belong to you."

She shook her head vigorously, making the ribbons of her *kapp* dance wildly. "I wasn't going to take anything. We already have one."

He eyed her suspiciously. "You already have what?"

"A new *bubbel*. Anne brought a little *brooder* to me last week. I just wanted to see how many more she had in her bag. I would rather have a sister if she has an extra one."

Joseph burst out laughing. "I'm afraid she doesn't have any more right now. You are going to have to keep your brother."

"Are you sure?"

"I'm sure."

The door to Anne's office opened, and she came out with a young woman who held a baby in her arms. He didn't recognize her. "I need to see the baby again in three weeks. Until then, enjoy him and have someone fetch me if you need anything else."

"I will, Anne. Have a nice day, and thanks for everything." The woman took her daughter by the hand and they left.

"I heard you laughing. What was so funny?"

"The little girl was trying to see how many more babies you have in your satchel."

Anne giggled. "Since Amish women don't discuss their pregnancies, the sudden appearance of a new sibling is sometimes confusing to children. I've had more than one try looking in my bag to see if I have others."

"I just stopped in to ask where you wanted your pumpkins stacked."

"Anywhere you want. It doesn't matter as long as they are close at hand for me. Can you bring a second load up, too?"

"I can." He left the house, unloaded what he had by the road and hurried back to the field. He was finally able to take a breather when he returned to the roadside stand with a second wheelbarrow full of freshly picked pumpkins. Anne was already there. He stopped in front of her and mopped the sweat from his brow on his sleeve.

Sitting inside the stand with Leah on her lap, Anne tipped her head as she regarded him. "Did you have trouble finding enough pumpkins?"

"*Nay*, only a little trouble with a goat this morning." He began unloading the wheelbarrow and stacked the pumpkins below the shelves in her stand.

"Nothing serious, I hope."

That made him pause in his work. He straightened with his hands on his hips. "Now you are worried about my goats? That's a switch."

She grinned. "Leah needs their milk. I will tolerate them because of that."

"You would like them all if you made the effort to get to know them."

"I'll take your word for it. Here comes a car. It's the first one all morning. I thought I would be busier, but maybe the folks that want pumpkins already have them." She was starting to worry that she wouldn't sell enough to cover her expenses for the season.

"Did the lady who wanted corn come back?"

Anne shook her head. "Not yet."

"Looks like your cornstalks will become livestock feed, after all. My goats will enjoy it."

"I'm not giving up on the lady. Keep your goats away until after November 1."

The car drove past without stopping. Anne's spirits drooped. "Don't bother picking more for now. We'll just have to haul them back if we don't sell them."

Sitting down on a straw bale beside her, he reached for Leah. "Don't give up. It's early yet."

She appreciated his encouragement. It was pleasant having company with her. Manning the stand was often a lonely task between customers. Having Joseph with her for companionship made the slow morning bearable.

More than bearable, Anne admitted. It was nice. They talked about a dozen different subjects. She had no idea he was interested in so many topics or that they liked so many of the same activities. He fished and so did she. He read books by many of the same authors she enjoyed. His goats might be his passion, but he was well-read and had an inquiring mind that surprised her. She was learning more than she ever thought possible about her reclusive neighbor. God had opened a door to Joseph using Leah as the key.

Two of their Amish neighbors drove past in their buggies. They waved but didn't stop. Anne waved back. Joseph didn't. She couldn't expect him to change completely overnight, but she was happy with the progress he had made.

The next vehicle that came down the road was their rural mail carrier. He leaned out his window with Anne's mail in his hand. "Morning, Miss Stoltzfus. I thought I should tell you that your sign by the highway is down. The county is working on the bridge just east of this road. It looks like they moved your sign to get their bulldozers down into the creek bed."

"Oh, dear. Perhaps that's why I haven't had any customers this morning. Thanks for letting me know, Mr. Potter."

"Don't mention it. Joseph, if I had known you were here, I would've brought your mail along."

Joseph perked up. "Was there a letter for me?"

"Nope. Just your newspaper and your *Goat World* magazine."

Anne watched the hope fade from Joseph's eyes. He was still waiting to hear from his sister. It was a letter Anne feared would never come.

"Have a nice day, folks." With a wave, the mail carrier drove off.

Anne sat beside Joseph and held out her copy of the paper for him to read. "I wonder if I should shut down early."

He handed Leah to her and took the paper. "I think that would be hasty. The sign has been there since the spring. People will have seen it before. If they want fresh produce, they will come this way."

"I reckon you're right. I will just have to wait and see how it goes."

She spent the next half hour playing with Leah before the baby grew tired and slept in her arms. The lady who wanted cornstalks returned just before noon. She took all the ones Anne had cut, explaining that they were being used to decorate a grade-school classroom with a harvest theme. She took an assortment of gourds and pumpkins, too, making Anne grateful that she hadn't closed the stand.

Joseph finished reading the paper and folded it neatly. "Do you have a cell phone?"

"I keep one in my midwife kit in case of an emergency. Why?"

"I wanted to make a call, but I'll go down the road to the Mast farm and use theirs."

Their *Englisch* neighbor lived less than a quarter of a mile away. A kindhearted elderly man, he was always willing to let the Amish use his phone. He was the one who kept Anne's spare cell phone batteries charged for her.

Joseph took off down the road without an explanation with the paper folded tightly in his hand. Anne spent the next hour cleaning the seeds from several of her overripe and damaged pumpkins. It was messy work, but she didn't mind. It was easiest to separate the seeds from the strands and mush by soaking them in a pail of water. The seeds floated to the top.

When Joseph returned, he grasped the handles of her wheelbarrow. "I'm going to gather a few more. You only have several dozen left in the field."

"You can if you wish, but I haven't sold a single one since you left."

"I think you'll sell all that you have." He

had such a sly smile on his face that she had to wonder what he was up to.

By late afternoon Joseph had delivered three wheelbarrow loads of the orange fruit to the roadside. Anne chafed at wasting her time waiting for customers who didn't show up. She had plenty to do to keep her busy in the house. "I think we should close, Joseph."

"I'd like to wait a little longer."

"Suit yourself, but I'm ready to go back to the house and so is Leah." The baby had been good all afternoon, but she was growing restless. Anne picked her up.

"Here come your next customers." Joseph took Leah from her.

Anne saw two pickups headed toward them. She was surprised when they both stopped. A teenage boy rolled down the passenger's-side window. "Is this the Stoltzfus pumpkin patch?"

"It is," Joseph called out.

"Sweet. This is it, guys. Load them up and be careful. We can't chunk broken ones. Make sure they're within the weight limit. If you have a doubt, Ben has a scale."

Anne watched in amazement as five young men swarmed her stand and began loading the trucks with her pumpkins.

"Are you taking them all?" This was astonishing. She wasn't sure what to think.

"All that we can find between eight and ten pounds," the one they called Ben said.

"What are you going to do with so many pumpkins?"

"We're going to chunk them."

She looked at Joseph. "Do you know what that means?"

He smiled and nodded. "It means they are going to load them onto a trebuchet and into air cannons and shoot them as far as possible."

Puzzled, she looked to the young men for an explanation. "What is a trebuchet?"

"It's a catapult," Ben said, weighing one of the questionable pumpkins on a small bathroom scale he had produced from the floor of his truck. "Half pound light. We can't take this one. You should come and watch. I hold the county record for the longest air-cannon shot."

Anne still wasn't sure what they were talking about.

Joseph chuckled. "I saw an article in the newspaper that said the Pumpkin Chunkin' Festival was getting under way in a few days. I called the number they had listed for information and asked if they needed more ammunition. It turns out they did."

"We're mighty glad you called. We need all the practice we can get. The big competition in Delaware is coming up in a couple of weeks. We plan to take home the grand prize," Ben said as he counted out the bills and handed them to Joseph.

Joseph held up one hand and nodded toward Anne. "The money goes to her. Keep us in mind for next year."

"We will, man. Good chunkin' pumpkins can be hard to find. Thanks for calling us." They all climbed into their trucks and took off.

As the dust settled, Anne stared in amazement at the money in her hand. It was far and above what she had expected to make for the entire season. She would be able to get a new wheelbarrow and order more seeds. She looked at Joseph. "You did this for me? How can I thank you?"

Without blinking an eye, he said, "You can help me milk the goats tomorrow."

"Are you kidding me?

The I-dare-you look in his eyes forced her to reconsider the answer hovering on the tip of her tongue.

Chapter Eleven

Joseph watched the play of emotions across Anne's expressive face. She didn't want to have anything to do with his goats, but she wasn't about to back out of her offer, either.

Her eyes narrowed and she crossed her arms tightly. "Very well. I will help you milk for one day."

"Both morning and evening."

She bowed her head in resignation. "I'll be there."

"Don't look so excited."

She shot him a sharp look. "I'm not."

He laughed heartily. Something he hadn't done in years. What was it about this woman that made him happy when he was talking to her, teasing her, just being near her? Had he avoided people for so long that the simplest exchange with a woman felt out of the ordinary and exciting?

Anne raised her chin. "Shall I take Leah now, or do you want to bring her over when you milk tonight?"

He grinned at the baby. "I'll keep her for a few hours."

"*Goot.* That will give me time to close up the stand. Shall I make her formula, or are you going to try making it yourself?"

"I reckon it's time I took over the task."

"I don't mind doing it."

"Are you sure?" He knew he could do it, but the chance to spend the evening with Anne was too good to pass up.

"You bring the raw milk and I'll have the rest ready, including supper. No arguments." She shook the money in the air. "This is cause for celebration. Pumpkin chunkin'! I never heard of such a thing."

After returning to his house, Joseph put Leah down for her nap and got started on the laundry that had piled up over the past week. When he had the last of it pinned on the clothesline, he fixed himself a cup of coffee and sat down to read his magazine. As interesting as the articles were, he couldn't keep his thoughts on supplement feeds with essential macro-and microminerals. His mind kept going back to the joy on Anne's face when she realized how much money her pumpkins had earned.

He enjoyed making her happy. Seeing her smile made him want to smile, too. The feeling was something he hadn't experienced in a long time. Not since Beth died.

Was it really almost thirteen years now since the accident? In a way, it felt as if it were only yesterday. So much of his life had changed in an instant.

He and Beth had been giddy teenagers, in a hurry to get started on a life together. Looking back, he realized now that he hadn't really known her. They had met at the wedding of a cousin in Delaware. For him it had been love at first sight. Beth had been as eager as he to marry. She'd come from a big family and wanted a home of her own.

She would've made him a good wife, and he would have been a good husband to her, but God had other plans for them.

Joseph realized he'd never looked for love again after her death. He didn't believe it could happen twice. He had been wrong about a lot of things. Maybe he was wrong about that, too.

He glanced at the baby sleeping in the crib beside his chair. If it hadn't been for Leah, he might have lived his whole life without getting to know Anne. What a shame that would've been.

Lord, You do move in mysterious ways. Help me to see the goodness in life and in the people around me. Make me a better servant to Your will.

When Leah woke from her nap, he changed her diaper and dressed her warmly. There was a distinct chill in the air. He noticed the wind had switched to the north as he carried the baby to Anne's house. She was waiting at the door for them. "The approaching winter is ready to make itself felt," she said, holding open the door.

"The paper had a hard freeze warning for this area."

"*Gott* has surely blessed me by holding off until now. I'm ready for some quiet days without weeds to hoe or produce to pick, sell or can."

He glanced at the array of pumpkins she

had lined up along the wall of her kitchen. "It doesn't look to me like you are done."

"A few dozen quarts of pumpkin puree won't take that long to make, but it sure will taste fine in soups, breads and pies this winter."

He eyed the pie pan on the counter. "Are we having a pie with supper?"

"Indeed we are. What better way to celebrate than with the fruits of our labors?"

"Sounds *goot*. I'll be back right quick."

Joseph left her house and hurried through his evening chores. At one point he found himself whistling. He paused in his work and gazed at the lights glowing in Anne's windows. He hadn't been this happy in a long time and she was the reason. If only Fannie would come home, his heart could truly be content.

Anne used a pair of thick hot pads to pull her pie from the oven. The mouthwatering aroma of pumpkin and spices filled the air. She took a deep breath and savored it. After setting the pie on the counter to cool, she checked the pork steaks simmering on the back burner and turned the heat down. All she needed now was to heat some of her freshly canned green beans and supper would be ready. She opened the pantry and pulled out a pint jar of them. She heard the front door open and a thrill of excitement jumped across her skin. "Come in. Supper will be ready in a few minutes."

"*Danki*, but we can't stay." It was a woman's voice.

Anne leaned back to look around her pantry door. Naomi Beiler and Bishop Andy stood inside her doorway. There was something in Naomi's expression that killed Anne's excitement.

"*Willkomm*. What brings you out here this evening?"

"I wanted to check on Joseph and the baby," the bishop said.

"After his less-than-cordial reaction to my last visit, I thought it was best that we check with you before we went to his home," Naomi added.

"They are both fine." Anne clutched the jar to her chest.

The bishop nodded but didn't take his eyes off her. "That's good to hear. This is an unusual situation."

Anne moved to the counter to open her green beans. "It is unusual, but Joseph is making the best of it. I watch the baby for him when he has to be away from the house."

"So he is paying you to be his *kindt heedah*?"

"Not paying exactly. He is doing some farm-work for me in exchange. He picked most of my pumpkins and that was a blessing."

"Several people mentioned seeing him with you at your roadside stand. Including Preacher Hostetler. I understand Joseph was there for several hours."

"*Ja*, he was." The jar lid came off with a pop. Anne poured the contents into a pan and set it on the burner. "Are you sure you can't stay for supper? I have plenty. Joseph will be here soon to pick up Leah. You can ask him then how he is doing."

"Your *karibs* pie smells *wunderbar*, but we have another visit to make yet tonight. They are expecting us to have supper with them."

"I see." She turned around and smoothed her apron. Joseph was standing behind the bishop with two pails of milk in his hands. He towered over the smaller man.

"*Guten owet*, Bishop. Naomi." Joseph set the buckets aside and pulled off his hat. He held it to his chest like a shield.

The bishop turned to him with a smile.

"Good evening to you, too, Joseph Lapp. We were just talking about you. How are you doing, my boy? I hear you have a niece staying with you."

"I do. Things are much better for us thanks to Anne and to the good ladies of Naomi's group who brought many fine gifts for us to use. You have been a true blessing, Naomi. *Danki*. Please share my thanks with the others."

The woman's face softened. "I'm glad to hear we have helped. It is what *Gott* wants us to do in His name."

Joseph looked at Anne. "Is Leah ready?"

"*Ja*, she is asleep in my office."

"*Danki*." He put his hat on, went through to the other room and returned a few moments later with the baby in his arms. "I will see you the same time tomorrow, Anne."

He wasn't staying for supper. "That's fine. I have to make a prenatal visit on Friday morning. I'll need you to pick Leah up by eight o'clock after your morning milking. Will that be a problem?"

"Not at all."

The bishop held the door open for him and the two men went out together.

Naomi stayed behind. She clasped her hands together. "You do not have a mother to tell you these things, so I hope you do not take it amiss that I am standing in her stead. You and Joseph can easily become food for gossip if you are seen being too familiar with one another."

Anne folded her arms tightly across her chest. "We haven't done anything improper."

"I'm sure of that. Just take care. A good reputation is easy to lose and hard to regain."

"People who gossip need to examine their own motives."

Naomi shook her head. "Do not be flippant, Anne. This is serious business. I'm looking out for you and for Joseph. He doesn't need to run afoul of public opinion. For now, he has the sympathy of many, but that can change. I'm sure the bishop is telling him the same thing I'm telling you."

"What would you have us do? He's my neighbor. I'm caring for his niece. We will see each other daily."

"Be circumspect. Don't be overly friendly, especially when you are in public. Limit your time together."

Anne bit the corner of her lip. She had encouraged Joseph's friendliness and enjoyed it more than she should. Maybe Naomi was right.

Naomi arched one eyebrow. "Unless he is courting you. In that case..."

"*Nay*, it is nothing like that," Anne added quickly.

"A pity. It would be a good match for the two of you and for the child. Tell my niece Rhonda when you see her that I will visit this coming Sunday. *Guten nacht*, Anne."

"Good night." Anne closed the door behind her and leaned against it. This wasn't the way she'd expected to end her evening. There would be plenty of leftovers for lunch tomorrow. She spied the pails of milk beside the door and carried them to a counter. Leah needed her formula whether her nanny was in trouble or not.

Anne slept poorly that night. She went over every moment she had spent in Joseph's company, looking for things that others might see as improper and wondering why she resented Naomi's advice. Naomi had her best interest at heart. Anne knew that.

When morning finally came, the light revealed heavy frost on the windowpanes. Was Joseph still expecting her to help milk his goats? She had no way of knowing. She would have to go ask. A sense of dread hung over her as she bundled up to go outside. Ending their friendship was the last thing she wanted to do.

She was almost to the gate between their properties when she saw him coming her way. He had Leah bundled in the baby quilt she had made. A pang of grief took her aback, but she suppressed it. The quilt had been made with love to keep a child warm. She was glad that child was Leah.

Joseph stopped on his side of the gate and spoke first. "I was bringing her to you."

The cautious expression in his eyes and his flat tone brought Anne's spirits to a new low. It seemed that the visit by the bishop and Naomi had indeed put an end to their budding friendship. She should take Leah and return to the house. That would be the circumspect thing to do.

Except Anne wasn't feeling particularly circumspect today. Joseph needed a friend. Asking her to turn her back on him was wrong. Would she rather have Joseph's friendship or Naomi's approval? "I thought you were going to teach me how to milk goats this morning."

"I don't think it would be a good idea."

"That's funny. I didn't think it was a good idea yesterday, but today I really want to learn."

He shook his head. "It wouldn't be proper. I don't wish to damage your reputation. The bishop is unhappy with us. Someone mistook our stumble into each other as a kiss. I set him straight."

That shocked her. "A kiss in public? You and I? That's ridiculous! Why would anyone believe such a tale?"

"I'm sure they don't any longer. I explained what happened."

"I should hope so."

"Now you see why helping me milk isn't a good idea."

"Joseph, I'm sure you received the same lecture that I did, or a very similar version. Goat milking wasn't mentioned to me. Was it mentioned to you?"

"You're splitting hairs, Anne."

"Am I? What if something were to happen to you? What if you fell and broke your leg? Who would take care of your goats? It's perfectly reasonable that I learn how." She softened her tone. "Besides, I really want to learn."

He stared at her for a long minute. Finally,

he rubbed his chin with one hand. "It does make sense that someone should know what to do if I'm laid up."

"Exactly."

"It might as well be you since you live closest."

Anne threw her hands wide. "*Ja*, I'm the logical choice."

"Except that you don't like my goats." A twinkle appeared in his eyes as a smile twitched at the corner of his lip.

Her heart grew light. This was the right thing to do. "All *Gottes* creatures deserve my respect and my care. Even goats. Even Chester."

She was rewarded with a bark of laughter from Joseph. "That's putting it on a little thick, Anne."

"I didn't sound sincere?"

"*Nay*, you didn't. Not at all." He handed her the baby and opened the gate so that she could come through.

"I'll work on it." She cast him a sassy look. Was he blushing?

They fell into step together as they walked toward his barn. He glanced her way. "You surprise me."

"Sometimes I surprise myself." Like now. Who would believe she was willingly going to milk a goat?

"I kind of like that about you."

Warmth flooded her and drove the cold from her cheeks. She was finding a lot of things she liked about Joseph, too, but she wasn't brave enough to tell him that. Not yet. He opened the gate to his pasture and Anne followed him in. He put his fingers to his mouth and whistled one piercing note. Seconds later dozens of animals came galloping toward them from all corners of the field.

They were about to be mobbed. Anne clutched Leah tightly to her chest and closed her eyes.

Chapter Twelve

When the expected impact didn't happen, Anne opened her eyes. She was surrounded by goats. Some were spotted, a few were snowy white, but the majority of them were brown with black markings. They milled around Joseph bleating softly. Some of them butted against his leg gently. Anne had seen them all in his pastures and a few of them in her garden, but Chester was the only one she'd been this close to.

One of the smaller white ones stood on her hind legs to investigate Anne. Another one tried to nibble on Leah's blanket. Anne held the baby higher. "Do they eat cloth?"

"Goats are browsers. They will sample about anything. They don't eat tin cans, though.

That is a myth, but they do enjoy eating the paper labels."

Anne noticed two of them had no ears. "What happened to these poor things? Did their ears freeze off? I've heard it can happen to animals in bad winters."

"Nothing happened to them. They are Lamanchas. They're an earless breed."

"How strange. Can they hear?"

"*Ja.* They have an ear canal same as any other. Ruby girl, *koom.*" He held out his hand and one of the white earless goats trotted over to nibble at his fingers.

"How many do you have?" Anne couldn't begin to count them, for they were all milling around.

"Over one hundred. I milk eighty of them. The rest are my breeding rams and a few of my kid crop from last spring that I haven't sold yet. I'm a seasonal pasture-based dairy. That means my does are bred in the fall and have their kids in the spring. Goats produce milk for about nine months. My milking season begins in March and ends in December each year. It gives my girls a two-month break to rest up before the next round of kids arrive. As soon as they freshen, I start milking again."

He scratched the head of the tall brown goat with a black line down her back. "This is Matilda. She is the matriarch of the group. They all follow her."

"Do they all have names?" A second goat tried to sample Leah's quilt. Anne pushed her away.

"*Ja*, I know them all by name. This is Jenny. She is my best producer. She gives me a full gallon morning and night. Matilda is her mother. The small buckskin-colored one chewing on your shoelace is her daughter Carmen. This is Zelda. This is Betsy. This is Cupcake. Over here is Yolanda." All of the females had heavy udders.

Anne cocked her eyebrow. "I'm not required to learn their names, am I?"

Joseph shrugged. "I reckon not, but they respond better when you call them by name."

Anne realized the musky odor of the does wasn't as strong as Chester's stink. "Why do the male goats smell so bad?"

"You don't want to know. They only smell bad to us. The female goats find the odor quite attractive."

"Then Chester must be a very popular fellow."

"He is," he said with a chuckle.

A pale brown doe with a white blaze on her face and droopy ears sniffed at Anne's hand. She was cute as a button. Anne smiled and tentatively petted her head. "Who is this?"

Joseph shifted his weight from one foot to the other, looking oddly ill at ease. "I thought you didn't want to learn their names."

Anne scratched the pretty doe behind the ear and the animal leaned into her hand, her eyes closed in bliss. "Not all of them. Just this one."

"It's Anne," he muttered so softly she almost didn't hear.

Anne's mouth dropped open. "Joseph Lapp, did you name a goat after me?"

"Not exactly. I try to go through the alphabet when I'm giving the new kids names and it was time for an *A* name."

"Annabel. Abigail. Arlene. There are lots of names that begin with *A*."

"I already have an Annabel and an Abigail. I picked Anne. It was no reflection on you."

She wasn't so sure, but she let the subject drop. "Show me how to milk."

"It's easy." He led the way inside his metal barn and flipped a switch.

The hum of a generator started up and in a few seconds, the lights came on. The building was large and airy with a high ceiling and white painted walls. Anne was amazed at how clean everything was. She didn't think of goats as clean animals.

"I noticed you use electricity."

"I have permission from the bishop to use it in my barn. I don't have it anywhere else on the farm. I use a propane-powered generator. It's cleaner than a diesel-fuel-powered one and less noisy. My goal is to produce the best goat's milk I can. An important part of that is keeping the milk clean and chilling it as soon as possible."

His milking parlor was a raised platform with twelve stanchions. The panels were painted royal blue and each place held a small blue tub in front of it. He climbed onto the platform and began filling the tubs from a small wheelbarrow. "I feed grain at milking time. The gals don't mind being milked, because they get fed."

When he had filled each tub, he opened the door at one end of the parlor. "*Koom*, girls. Up you go."

The goats filed in quickly. They walked up one ramp to come into the parlor. Another ramp led down and out of the barn. The first doe walked all the way to the end of the line before stopping and putting her head in the stanchion. Each one did the same until all the places were full. As each goat began eating, Joseph closed the latches that would keep their heads locked in place.

He hopped off the platform and stood beside Anne. "It's important to clean their udders thoroughly with an iodine solution and dry them well before putting on the suction tubes. The milk goes directly from the goat into the milker, then into a pipeline, through a filter and finally to the milk tank in the next room, where it is chilled in a holding tank. A truck comes three times a week to pick up the milk."

"How long does it take?"

"To milk all of them? It takes me about two hours."

"How do you clean all this tubing?"

He began washing the udders of each doe and attaching the milkers. "I'll show you when I'm done. The pipeline system gets cleaned after each milking, morning and night. Warm water flushes the leftover milk out of the lines. That is followed by a hot-water detergent rinse and then a mild bleach rinse. Like in the house,

I have a propane hot-water heater here. The milk lines are sanitized just prior to each milking."

This was a much more complex operation than she had imagined. "Joseph, none of this looks easy except opening the door and letting them in."

"It looks more complicated than it is. You'll get the hang of it in no time."

She shifted the baby to her other hip. "I agreed to help do this for one day."

He leaned on the parlor ramp. "I remember. When do you want to start?"

"Haven't we started already?"

"I'm showing you how it's done. You haven't helped me do anything yet. Are you backing out of our deal? I did manage to sell almost all your pumpkins." He moved toward her and took Leah from her.

"You did and I'm not backing out. I'm grateful for your help. I will attempt milking one evening, with your supervision, of course."

"Of course. I don't trust my gals to just anyone. Isn't that right, Leah?" He bounced the baby and smiled at her. She grinned back at him.

Anne cocked her head to the side as she

watched him interact with Leah. He was a much different man from the sour, reclusive neighbor she had lived next to for so many years. It did her heart good to see such a positive change in him.

Joseph caught Anne looking at him with a soft smile on her lips and tenderness in her eyes. His heart started beating faster. His logical mind quickly quelled the sensation. Her tender smile was aimed at the baby and not at him. He shouldn't read more into her friendliness than was there. He knew he had to keep their relationship casual or he'd risk running into problems with the church community. He wouldn't do anything to jeopardize Anne's reputation.

"I've shown you how the milking is done. I reckon that's good enough. Why don't you take Leah back to your house? I think she's ready for a nap." He didn't mean to sound brusque, but his words came out that way. He handed her the baby.

Anne's smile faded. "I will see you later."

He didn't want her to go, but he had no reason to stop her. He waited until she reached the door. "Anne?"

She turned back to face him. "Yes?"

He wanted to say, *Don't go*. Instead, he asked, "What do you think of my goats now?"

Her smile reappeared. "I still like them much better when they are on your side of the fence."

"Now that the growing season is over, would you consider letting me graze them in your fields? For a price."

"How much of a grazing fee are you offering?"

He gave her a price that was less than what it would cost him to buy the same amount of feed.

"I'll think it over."

"What's to think about? You get your fields cleared and I get low-cost feed for my gals that's right next door."

"If you want to graze it, there may be others in the area who would like to graze it, too. Maybe someone else will pay me more. As I said, I'll think it over. Cows and sheep will eat the broken and blemished pumpkins that are still out there. They will eat the leaves and vines, too."

If she was looking to foster the appearance of a business relationship with him for propriety's sake, he understood. "Ask around. I doubt you will get a better price."

"I *will* ask around. If I decide not to let your goats graze it, will you complain about me?"

"Loudly, and to everyone who will listen."

"That settles it," she said primly and left without giving her answer.

He chuckled as he returned to work. Anne certainly wasn't a boring woman. Her self-sufficient streak might have been what kept her single all these years. Each day he seemed to discover something new and intriguing about his bossy neighbor.

And each day he liked her more.

He pushed the thought aside. For Leah's sake, he valued Anne's friendship, but he knew there would never be anything more between them. He was a bachelor set in his ways. She was bent on remaining single. It wouldn't work between them.

So why was he even thinking about it?

He gave himself a sharp mental shake and went to feed Chester. To his chagrin, he discovered the buck was missing. Again. Somehow he had escaped from the stall.

A quick check of the outbuildings showed the goat wasn't on the farm. Joseph headed to

Anne's, praying the goat wasn't causing any new damage. His prayer went unheeded. He found Chester in the corral chasing Anne's mare away from her hay. The old goat was leaping and kicking happily in the crisp morning air, making the frightened horse dash from one end of the enclosure to the other.

"Chester, *koom*! Before Anne sees your mischief and I end up in her bad graces again." He managed to shepherd the goat home, found where he had worked a board loose to get out and fixed it.

As he hammered the last nail in place, he glared at Chester. "At least Anne wasn't the one to find you. You have to stop giving her a bad impression of goats. Behave. We want her to like us."

Joseph straightened as soon as the words were out of his mouth. He did want Anne to like him because he cared about her. A lot.

It was a scary thought.

On Friday morning Anne walked out to hitch up her horse a little after eight o'clock. When the mare came limping toward her, Anne frowned in concern.

"You poor thing. What's wrong?"

Anne slipped into the corral to examine Daisy's right front leg. Her knee was swollen and hot. Anne patted the mare's neck. "You aren't going to carry me to the Yoder farm this morning. You are going to have to rest for a few days. I'll fix up a poultice for you as soon as I get back."

Leaving the corral, Anne headed to Joseph's house. She found him mending a pair of socks at the kitchen table. "Good morning, Joseph."

"*Wee gayt's*, Anne. What can I do for you?"

"I'm sorry to bother you, but I wonder if I might borrow your buggy horse this morning. My mare has come up lame."

He laid his mending aside. "Do you want me to look at her for you? Maybe it's just a loose shoe."

"It's her right knee. She has had some trouble with it in the past. She must have twisted it while she was out in the pasture because I haven't used her since last Sunday. I won't be gone long. Rhonda Yoder is expecting me at nine o'clock. Prenatal visits normally take about thirty minutes."

"You can't borrow my horse."

Stunned, she drew back. "Oh."

"I'll drive you." He got his coat and hat.

"That's not necessary."

"Duncan is temperamental. I wouldn't want him to run away with you. If you will get Leah ready, I will go hitch him up."

"All right."

Within ten minutes Anne had the heavily bundled baby in her Moses basket and was standing outside waiting for Joseph. She handed him the baby and then climbed in. Once she was settled, she took Leah and placed the basket next to them on the seat.

Joseph flicked the reins and set the horse in motion. "You will have to tell me how to get there. I haven't been to their place since they moved."

"They live on the west side of Honeysuckle now."

"Okay." He turned the horse in that direction when he reached the end of the lane.

Anne enjoyed riding beside Joseph until they reached the edge of town. Several of the women from Naomi's widows' group were gathered in front of the Beachy Craft Shop. Their curious looks and furious whispering made Anne realize how odd it must look for her to be riding out with Joseph only a day after Naomi and the bishop had come to call.

She resisted the urge to pull her traveling bonnet low across her face.

"I should have come alone," she muttered.

"Why?"

"People are staring at us." It was one thing to defy Naomi's suggestion to be more circumspect with Joseph when they were alone on their farms. It was another thing to brazenly disregard that advice in front of her church members.

"They will soon find other things to talk about."

Anne wasn't so sure. She may have opened herself up to criticism for no reason. Duncan was behaving perfectly. She could have handled him easily. Why hadn't she thought about being seen with Joseph?

Because she wanted his company and that was as far ahead as she had been thinking.

Joseph glanced at her. "It will be fine. You'll see. We will explain what happened. After everything you have done for me, it's nice to be able to do something for you in return. Besides, it's sort of my fault that your mare is lame."

"How can that be?"

"Yesterday one of my goats got in with her

and was chasing her. That may have been when she hurt her leg."

Anne narrowed her eyes at him. "Let me guess. It was Chester."

"Ja," Joseph admitted with a hangdog expression.

"That miserable animal. I don't know why you put up with him."

Duncan chose that moment to shy violently as a dog ran across the road in front of them. Anne toppled into Joseph. He threw his arm around her and pulled her to his side to steady her. She looked up in gratitude. Her heart hammered in her chest, not from fear but from his nearness. *"Danki."*

Another buggy topped the rise in front of them. Anne knew exactly who it was before they got close enough to see the driver. She struggled out of Joseph's embrace, pushing his arm off her shoulder. It was the bishop's buggy.

Joseph acknowledged him with a tip of his hat. The bishop's countenance remained set in disapproval.

Anne wanted to sink through the seat. "Just so you know, I'm going to plant rhubarb the entire length of our property line in the spring."

"I can't say that I blame you."

She could tell from the tone of his voice that he was worried now, too.

Chapter Thirteen

The road remained free of traffic for the next mile as Anne and Joseph traveled on. It should have been a pleasant morning drive through the rolling hills of Lancaster County. Autumn colors splashed the tree-covered hillsides with scarlet, golds and flaming oranges. The harvest was finished. The land and the people who worked it were ready to rest. Shocks of corn lined up like brown tepees across the fields, waiting to be used when snow covered the ground. The orchards were bare. The pasture grasses were turning brown, though the cattle and horses still foraged there.

The air had a nip to it and held the scent of wood smoke rising from the Amish farms they passed. The sun shone brightly, promising a warm afternoon. There wasn't a cloud in the sky.

Joseph glanced at Anne several times, but she refused to look at him. "I will go see the bishop first thing tomorrow morning and explain that this was an unusual occurrence. I was simply doing my Christian duty by offering you assistance."

"I should've had you stop at the Beachy Craft Shop. I should have asked one of the women there to take me out to the Yoder farm. I wasn't thinking. I know what's proper."

"There's no harm done. Tongues may wag about us for a day or so, but when we give them nothing else to talk about, this will be forgotten."

Anne sat up straighter. "You're right. We aren't doing anything wrong. I have nothing to be ashamed of this time."

This time? What did that mean? Had she done something to be ashamed of in the past? Sadness stole over her features as a faraway look entered her eyes.

"Is something wrong, Anne?" He wanted to help, to comfort her, but he didn't know how.

She shook her head and the distant look disappeared. "Nothing's wrong. About a mile farther on, you'll cross a bridge. The Yoder home is on the south side of the road."

They soon caught up to a wagon loaded with hay traveling in the same direction. When he could safely do so on the hilly highway, Joseph passed it, urging Duncan to a burst of speed. The moment the black horse came neck and neck with the draft horses, he broke trot and tried to gallop ahead of them.

Anne clutched Leah's basket with white knuckles until Joseph was able to regain control. Her eyes were wide with fright. "I see what you mean about your horse being hard to handle."

"He came from a racing farm. He does well most of the time, but now you see why I didn't want you to drive him alone."

"I do, and I'm grateful you insisted on coming."

They rode in silence for a while longer. Suddenly he asked, "Do you like being a midwife?"

"I don't like it. I love it. I love mothers and their incredible strength. I love babies and their amazing resiliency. It's a humbling part of life and I'm blessed to play a role in it."

"Did you have to have a lot of training?"

"I am what is known as a direct-entry midwife. I am not a nurse. I don't have a nursing license, but I am a CPM. That stands for *certified professional midwife*. It means I have met the requirements for those credentials. My mother was a midwife for many years in Ohio. I apprenticed with her. After I moved here, I joined an association of midwives that work to improve the training and practice of midwifery. They hold workshops and classes several times a year. Although I do mainly home births, I can do deliveries at the birthing center attached to the hospital."

"I don't know much about midwives."

"I'm not surprised. I follow the Midwives Model of Care. That means I monitor the physical, emotional and social well-being of women during their childbearing years. I provide individualized education and prenatal care. I'm there to provide continuous hands-on assistance while a mother is in labor, during delivery and in the months after the baby is born. My goal is to help a woman understand that birth is a natural process that does not require technological intervention except in very rare cases."

"How many babies have you delivered?"

"Thirty-six in the last three years," she said, pleased with her success.

"That's not so many. I was at the delivery of forty-four kids last spring alone. I'd hate to try to count the number since I raised my first goat."

She shook her head in disbelief. "I think goats are a little different from human mothers and babies."

"Nope. We're more alike than you want to believe."

She didn't rise to his bait. He wanted to get her mind off the bishop's disapproval, but she wouldn't let him.

They reached the Yoder farm without further incident. Anne went inside while he waited in the buggy with Leah. The baby was still sleeping. It was warm in the sun and he wasn't worried about her getting a chill. Silas Yoder came out of the barn. He waved when he saw Joseph and came over to speak to him. The two of them had attended all eight grades together in the one-room schoolhouse not far from the outskirts of Honeysuckle, but Silas had joined a different church district when he married Rhonda. The two men rarely saw each other now.

"Long time no see. What brings you to my place today, Joseph?"

"I brought Anne Stoltzfus to see your wife. Her horse came up lame this morning. She wanted to borrow my buggy horse so she wouldn't be late, but Duncan is temperamental. I decided it was safer to drive her."

Silas winked. "As good an excuse as any to take a *maidel* out for a drive on a nice day. Anne is a sweet one. I've often wondered why she remains unwed. She's not hard on the eyes. Who is that you have with you?" He leaned in to get a better look at the baby.

Joseph tensed. He had been dreading this. He knew he would have to introduce his niece to the community and tell her story sooner or later. He was surprised that Silas hadn't already heard about his sister's actions. News traveled amazingly fast among the Amish in spite of their lack of telephones. "This is Leah. She is Fannie's daughter."

"You don't say? How is your sister? Has she returned?"

It had been more than three weeks since Fannie had dropped Leah in his lap and over two weeks since her only letter arrived. It should have been more than enough time for her to come to her senses and return for Leah. Or at least to write and ask how the babe was doing.

He didn't want to believe she could abandon her child, but how much longer could he pretend she was coming back?

"My sister has left our faith. I do not know when I will see her again."

"I'm sorry to hear that, Joseph. I will pray for her. She has a pretty *bubbel*. I can't believe I'm going to have one of my own in a few weeks. Do they really wake up and cry every two or three hours through the night?"

"They do. Through the day, too."

"Every night?"

"Every night until they decide otherwise."

Silas shook his head. "I don't think I'm ready for this, Joseph. How can I be a *vadder*? I'm not a smart man, not like my *daed*. He knows a little about everything. There's nothing he can't fix. I tell you, I'm worried about bringing a child up who will embrace our faith. What if my son or daughter is as wild during their *rumspringa* as I was during mine?"

Joseph thought of all Anne had taught him about caring for Leah. "I reckon you must pray for guidance. You have a good wife, Silas. Listen to her. She will help you become a *goot vadder*. If your children give you gray hairs, it is only right. I remember how your *mudder* worried over you."

Silas grinned. "She still does.

"It's the way of the world."

Silas glanced toward the house and his smile faded. "I'll be glad when this pregnancy is over. Rhonda worries me more every day. She thinks something is wrong with the babe, and I can't convince her otherwise."

Anne could see that Rhonda wasn't feeling well as soon as she entered the house. The young mother-to-be wore a pained expression and rubbed her stomach almost constantly. Anne sought to calm her and find out what was wrong.

It didn't take long for Rhonda to voice her concerns. "The baby isn't moving much. Shouldn't the baby be more active now?"

Warning bells went off in Anne's mind but she kept her face calm. "The quarters are getting tighter for your little one. He or she may not have as much room to wiggle. Let's get you checked out. You may be closer to your delivery date than I thought."

Anne weighed Rhonda on the bathroom

scale she carried with her and jotted down the numbers on the record book she kept for each of her patients. She also checked her blood pressure and her pulse. It was all normal. "Your weight has stayed the same."

"I don't know how it can. I feel as big as a cow. I had to have Silas help me out of the bathtub the other night. It was so embarrassing."

"I'm sure he didn't mind."

"*Nay*, he's been a great help and so understanding. I've been blessed with a wonderful husband."

Anne pulled out her stethoscope. "I agree. Lie down on the bed for me and let me take a listen to your little one."

"Do you think it will be a boy or a girl? *Mam* says I'm carrying the babe low, so it will be a boy. Is that true?"

"It is about fifty percent of the time," Anne said with a wink and a grin. She put the bell of the stethoscope to Rhonda's belly. Her grin faded. The heartbeat she heard was much too slow. She listened in a different place and found the same results.

"Turn on your left side, Rhonda."

"Why? What's wrong?" She rolled over.

Anne listened again. The heartbeat was a shade faster, but not normal. "Stay on your side for a few minutes."

"Something is wrong. I can see it on your face. What is it? Tell me!" Tears welled up in Rhonda's eyes.

Anne knew that overwhelming sense of panic and fear as well as she knew her own name. She drew a deep breath. "You must keep calm. It's important. The baby's heart rate is slow."

"But it's there?"

"*Ja*, it's there. It gets better when you are on your side. I want you to stay this way while I talk to Silas. I'm going to suggest that you go to the hospital."

"But I want my baby born at home," she wailed.

Anne grasped Rhonda's hand and gave it a reassuring squeeze. "I know you do and going to the hospital now doesn't mean that can't happen. But I'm concerned. I think you should see a doctor. He can take a look at the baby with an ultrasound and see what is causing the problem."

"Talk to Silas. We can't afford a hospital bill. Is *Gott* taking my baby away?"

"I pray that is not His plan." She didn't want any young mother to suffer the pain of a still-born child.

"You know I can't make this decision, Anne. I must be obedient to my husband."

"I understand. I'll be right back. Okay?"

Rhonda nodded and Anne hurried outside. *This can't be happening. Please, God, don't let this baby die. Not the way my baby did.*

She saw Silas talking to Joseph and rushed to him. She hated to frighten the young man, but she had no choice. "Silas, I must speak with you."

He grew instantly somber. "What is it?"

She had to keep calm. Everyone was depending on her. She prayed for strength. "I have examined Rhonda, and I discovered that your baby's heartbeat is slower than normal."

"What does that mean?" Worry filled his eyes.

"It means the baby is in distress. Something isn't right. I'm going to urge you to take Rhonda to the hospital."

"Is she losing our baby?" Fear replaced the worry on his face.

"I can't say for sure, but that may happen."

He pulled off his hat and raked a hand

through his hair. "If it is *Gottes* will to take my child back to Heaven, I must accept His will. *Gott* help me to be strong."

She clutched his arm. "Silas, listen to me. Every minute counts. If it is *Gottes* will to call your babe home, nothing we do will change that. But *Gott* in His wisdom brought me here today for a reason. Maybe that reason was to see the danger and send you both to the hospital. I need your permission to call the ambulance. The church will help with the hospital bills. You know that."

"I don't care about the money. Call the ambulance." He ran toward the house.

Anne staggered toward the buggy and felt her knees give way.

Joseph jumped down in time to catch Anne as she slumped against him. "Are you all right?"

She nodded but didn't speak as she clutched his arms.

"Tell me what you need me to do. How can I help?"

She focused on his face. "I'm so frightened for them."

"*Gott* is with us all. We can bear what must be borne. Rhonda and Silas, too."

"I know." She drew several deep breaths.

"Shall I call for the ambulance?"

She shook her head. "I can do that. I need you to go out to the highway and direct them here when they arrive."

He leaned forward to peer into her eyes. "Are you sure you don't need me here?"

She managed a wan smile. "I'm okay now. I have a patient to take care of."

"*Goot* girl. Make the call. I'll go out to the highway as soon as I know they are on their way."

Leah woke and began to fuss. Joseph picked her up to quiet her. Anne pulled a cell phone from her apron pocket and flipped it open to dial 911. When the dispatcher answered, she explained the situation and gave concise medical information about Rhonda, answered the dispatcher's questions and provided directions. When she was finished, she closed the phone. "I'm going back inside. The ambulance should be here in ten minutes."

"Then I'm on my way. I will keep Leah with me so you are free to do what you need."

"Bless you, Joseph. I'm so glad you are here."

"I wish I could do more." He settled Leah in her Moses basket again, climbed in beside her and slapped the reins against Duncan's back. The horse jumped forward and Joseph guided him down the road to the highway. After that, he had to sit and wait. Thankfully, Anne had packed a bottle for Leah and he was able to feed the baby. She was almost finished when he heard the sound of a siren in the distance. He climbed out of the buggy, then walked to the edge of the roadway and began waving his arm when he saw the flashing lights crest the hill.

The ambulance slowed. He motioned toward the Yoder farm. The ambulance driver nodded that he understood and turned onto the dirt track. Joseph got back in his buggy and followed them.

The paramedics were already pulling a gurney from the back of the ambulance when he arrived. Knowing he could help by staying out of the way, he waited and prayed for everyone in the farmhouse. Twenty minutes later the paramedics brought Rhonda out on a gurney and loaded her into the ambulance. She lay on her side. Her face was pale and streaked with tears. She had a green oxygen mask over her nose and mouth. Silas was at her side holding her hand. He looked every bit as pale and shaken as she did. He climbed in the ambulance when they had her loaded, and the doors were closed.

Three additional buggies drove into the yard. Joseph wasn't surprised. The unusual sound of an ambulance in the normally quiet farm country would bring neighbors hurrying to see if they could help.

Then the ambulance pulled away, leaving Joseph to answer the many questions of Silas and Rhonda's friends. He waited for Anne to appear, but she didn't come out of the house. When the last of the curious neighbors departed to spread the word of what was going on, Joseph walked up to the house, looking for Anne. Inside, he found her huddled in a rocker with her arms clasped around her knees, sobbing.

Chapter Fourteen

"Don't cry. Please don't cry, Anne. You did everything you could."

The sound of Joseph's voice penetrated Anne's sorrow. She opened her eyes to see him kneeling in front of her. Through the blur of her tears, she saw the concern etched on his face. How could she tell him the tears weren't for Rhonda and her baby but for a baby boy, stillborn and laid to rest years ago? They were tears she had kept at bay for fifteen long years, but today's events brought back every bitter, sad memory of that time in sharp detail. It was exactly what had happened to Anne, but her mother had never called for the ambulance.

Anne tried to but couldn't speak. She reached out and laid her palm against Joseph's face. He cupped his hand over hers and held it tight.

"We should go home now," he said softly. "Are you ready?"

Her hiccuping sobs slowed. Finally, she nodded.

Joseph helped her to her feet and kept one arm around her. She cherished his strength. Although she was used to standing alone, today she needed someone to lean on. She needed him.

He helped her into the buggy after scooting Leah over to make room so that Anne could sit beside him. She should have objected, but she didn't. She was emotionally spent. The comfort of Joseph's touch meant more to her than proper behavior.

Picking up the reins, he set the horse in motion. Anne kept her eyes closed as she leaned against him.

"Is there any hope for Rhonda's babe?" he asked a short time later.

Sighing, Anne sat up. Immediately, she missed the warmth of his body. "The baby's heartbeat improved when they put the oxygen mask on Rhonda. I imagine the doctor will do an emergency C-section when they reach the hospital. If *Gott* wills it, the child will live."

"I'm relieved to hear that. From the force of your weeping, I thought the babe had perished."

She wanted to tell him about her baby, but shame kept her silent. It was a shame she had hidden for many years. Only her mother and the maiden aunt Anne had stayed with in Ohio knew about her unwed pregnancy. Anne had been seventeen at the time. Seventeen, headstrong and in love. As it turned out, she couldn't marry the *Englisch* boy she adored. He hadn't loved her. He hadn't wanted to be a father. He'd urged her to give the baby up for adoption. Her mother had thought it would be best, too.

Brokenhearted, she had agreed to give her baby to a childless Amish couple in her aunt's church. She'd never imagined she would have to give him back to God. A single question haunted her still. If she had been brave enough to keep her son, would God have allowed it?

Joseph watched her closely. She wouldn't share her story, not even with him. "I was just overwrought. I keep thinking I must have missed something. I didn't foresee Rhonda having any problems. I was frightened, but I tried not to let them see that. I'm sorry I fell apart."

"Are you better now?"

"I am. I'm fine." She scrubbed her face with her hands to erase the signs of her tears and sniffed once.

"You don't seem fine." He pulled her close again.

Laying her head on his shoulder, she relaxed in his embrace. Did he know how wonderful it felt to be cared for? Did he have any idea how firmly he was planting himself in her heart?

It was time to admit she was falling for this man. She understood he offered the kindness of a friend, but the feelings swirling through her were more than friendship. Unless she was very careful, she would find herself in love with another man who didn't love her in return.

She sat up straight, determined to put their relationship back on proper footing. "We should stop and let Naomi know what has happened."

"That's a *goot* idea. You can explain why we were driving out together this morning, too. Naomi will put a stop to any gossip about us if you fill her in on the details."

"You might be right about that. What about the Yoders' bishop? Should we tell him what's going on?"

"A number of neighbors came by when the ambulance was there. I'm sure he already knows."

Anne had to chuckle. "There's nothing quite as fast and efficient as the Amish telegraph."

And sometimes completely inaccurate, as in the case of their "kiss." Casting a quick glance his way, she wondered, *What would it be like to kiss him?*

It was best not to think such thoughts. She lifted Leah's infant carrier to her lap, scooted away from Joseph and placed the baby between them. They remained quiet for the rest of the trip. The streets of Honeysuckle were empty, so Anne didn't have to face any of her friends again. For that she was thankful. She knew her blotchy, tear-streaked face wouldn't go unnoticed.

Joseph turned the horse into Naomi's driveway and stopped in front of her house. Her fourteen-year-old daughter, Abigail, was sweeping the front steps. She smiled brightly. *"Wee gayt's."*

Anne stepped out of the buggy. "Good day to you, too, Abigail. Is your *mudder* about?"

"*Ja, koom* in." Abigail's eyes filled with concern. Anne knew she must look a sight with her red eyes and blotchy cheeks.

"I'll only be a minute." She glanced at Joseph.

He nodded. "I'll wait here."

She followed Abigail inside and found Naomi at her quilting rack. Naomi smiled. "Anne, I wasn't expecting you. Come in. Pick up a needle. Child, have you been crying?"

"I'm afraid I bring you some unhappy news."

Concern furrowed Naomi's brow. "What is it?"

"I saw Rhonda today. I've sent her to the hospital. Her baby wasn't doing well."

"Oh, my poor child. I must go at once to see what I can do." She slipped her needle into the fabric and got up.

"I thought you would want to know right away. Can you get word to Silas's family?"

"I can. *Danki*, Anne. It was good of you to stop. Would you like a cup of tea or coffee? I'll have Abigail fix something."

"*Nay*, I can't stay. My mare came up lame this morning and Joseph was kind enough to drive me to see Rhonda. He and Silas went to school together. I've already kept Joseph from his work long enough. I must go."

"Thank you again for stopping. Please tell Joseph I'm grateful for his kindness to you."

"I will."

Anne left the house knowing she had done all she could to quiet the gossip about Joseph and herself and to let Rhonda's family know what was happening. Joseph held out a hand to help her into the buggy. He had Leah in his arms. She was crying.

"I'll take her," Anne said, letting him have free hands to drive.

"I couldn't find another bottle."

"I only packed one. I thought we'd be home long before this." She cuddled Leah close. The baby stopped crying and grabbed the ribbon of Anne's *kapp*. She pulled the material to her mouth and gurgled happily.

Anne smiled at her. If she was in danger of falling for Joseph, she had already gone over that cliff with Leah. It would be impossible not to love such a sweet child. Anne kissed the baby's hand. Leah was becoming as dear to her as her own babe would have been. Why had

Fannie chosen to give her baby away? Anne wanted to know. She wanted to understand.

Yet forgiveness did not require understanding. She forgave Fannie and prayed that Joseph had forgiven her, too.

Joseph kept a close eye on Anne as they traveled home. It was distressing to see her so sad and not be able to help her. He could believe she was upset by Rhonda's emergency, but he didn't believe that was all that was troubling her. There was something else. Something she didn't want to share with him. He noticed that she held Leah close, stroking her face, holding her hand, kissing her tiny fingers. It was as if only Leah could give Anne the solace she needed.

He drove her up to the front door of her home. She remained seated, as if she didn't want to be parted from the baby. "Anne, could I ask you a favor?"

"Of course." She glanced at him. There were still traces of tears on her cheeks.

"I'm going to be working late tonight. I have to take apart all my milking lines and replace some of the O-rings. I've noticed that I have less suction than I should. I'm just not sure where the trouble is. Would you keep Leah overnight for me? I know that's not our usual arrangement."

Anne stared at him intently. A tender smile appeared on her face. "You are a good friend to me, Joseph Lapp."

He didn't mind that she saw through his ruse. He would work late. One of his O-rings did need replacing. It wouldn't hurt him to catch up on his paperwork, either. "You are a good friend to me, too. Can you keep her?"

Anne kissed the baby's cheek. "Of course I will."

"Danki." He leaned over and placed a gentle kiss on Anne's cheek. Her eyes widened, but she didn't pull away. He tried to tell himself it was a gesture of friendly comfort, but he realized he was only lying to himself. He had come to care deeply about Anne. Much more deeply than he should care about someone who was simply his neighbor.

She placed Leah in her basket. He got out and lifted her down. He set the baby on the ground and reached for Anne. His hands easily spanned her waist. She rested her hand slightly on his shoulders as he lowered her to the ground. She gazed up at him with wide eyes. It took a strong act of willpower not to kiss her again.

He reluctantly stepped away. Anne picked up the baby carrier and walked up her steps. At the door, she turned to look back at him. "Thank you again for everything you did today."

He tried to make light of it. "It is my Christian duty to help my neighbor."

"This neighbor is grateful that she lives next door to a kind and caring man."

"Even if he is a goat farmer?"

That brought a little smile to her lips. "*Ja*, even if he is a goat farmer. With poor fences."

"I can see my welcome is just about worn through. I'll talk to you tomorrow morning." He tipped his hat and led his horse toward the gate between their properties. As he closed it behind the buggy, he noticed the hinge was loose and the wire was starting to sag. If she believed him to be a kind and caring neighbor, then he had better start living up to her expectations.

Anne fed Leah and put her down in a small playpen Joseph had provided her from the donated items at his place. As soon as she was done, she sat down in the kitchen and pulled out her cell phone. She hesitated but finally dialed the number to the obstetrical unit at their local hospital. Anne was relieved when her friend Roxann answered the phone. Roxann was a nurse-midwife who taught classes for the Amish midwives in the area. Anne had learned a lot from Roxann and valued her as a friend.

"*Hallo*, Roxann. This is Anne Stoltzfus. I'm calling to check on my patient Rhonda Yoder. She was brought in by ambulance this morning. Can you give me an update?"

"Let me check to make sure she has signed a release to give you information, Anne. You know how picky the HIPAA laws are. Yes, it's here on her chart. I'm happy to say that mother and baby boy are both doing well. We did a crash C-section for low heart tones as soon as she arrived. The baby had the cord wrapped around his neck three times. He was very fortunate that you saw his mother today. The proud papa has been singing your praises to everyone who will listen."

Ann clapped a hand to her chest as relief brought tears to her eyes again. *Thank You, God, for sparing this woman and child.*

She had prepared herself to hear the worst. Instead, she was overcome with gratitude and joy. "I'm so thankful. *Gott es goot.*"

"I don't speak *Deitsch*, but I get your meaning, Anne. Our new obstetrician was impressed with the medical records you sent along with the EMS staff and your handling of the patient. You did exactly the right thing. He's one of those doctors who think Amish midwives don't know how to read or write, let alone deliver babies."

"Was there anything in my records that I missed? Should I have known this might be a problem?" The day had shaken her belief in her calling. Was she meant to be a midwife?

"A nuchal cord doesn't normally have warning signs until the baby drops lower in the birth canal and the cord gets tight. You didn't miss anything. You did good getting Rhonda into a position that took pressure off the cord and in sending her to the hospital as soon as you discovered there was a problem."

It made Anne feel better that she hadn't missed something, but her spirits remained low. What about the next time a mother had problems? Would she be skilled enough to handle it?

"Rhonda and her baby should be dismissed in about three days," Roxann said.

"I will follow up with them as soon as they get home."

"Thanks for making our direct-entry midwife program look good. We still have some resistance in the medical community, but you and I both know home births are every bit as safe as a hospital birth. If they weren't, there wouldn't be so many Amish babies in Pennsylvania. Rhonda was the exception to the rule, but a sharp midwife knows when to call for help. You are a sharp midwife, Anne."

"It was in *Gottes* hands. I only did what I have been trained to do. I appreciate the information, Roxann. Call me if anything changes."

"I will. How many of your mothers are due in November?"

"Only two in November now, but four in January."

"You're going to be busy. Have a happy Thanksgiving, if I don't talk to you before then."

Anne closed her phone and tucked it into her case. Now that the crisis was over, she felt weak as a kitten. She fixed herself a cup of tea and went to sit in the rocker in her office. She stayed there for an hour watching Leah sleep. In her heart, Anne knew Rhonda would be doing the same thing. She would be watching her baby slumber and giving thanks to God for His mercy.

She wasn't surprised when Joseph showed up as daylight was fading. Leah was awake. Anne was holding her and reading her a story. He stepped into her office and pulled off his hat. "Have you heard anything?"

"They had to do a C-section but mother and baby are fine. I should have come to tell you that. I'm sorry."

Relief filled his eyes. *"Gott es goot."*

"*Ja, Gott* is good. He showed us all His power and His mercy today. Would you like some supper?"

"*Nay,* I've eaten. I don't want to intrude on your evening. I just wanted to know how things turned out. You look better."

"Was I haggish before?"

His gaze softened and he shook his head. "Only tired and worried looking. I doubt you could look haggish if you tried."

"That is sweet of you to say." Her grumpy neighbor wasn't so grumpy, after all. She was coming to depend on him, on his kindness and his insight.

A flush crept up his neck and he ducked his head to avoid her gaze. "It's the truth, that's all. Would you like me to take Leah home?"

She gazed at the baby on her lap. Leah was grasping at the colorful pictures on the pages of the children's book. "If you don't mind, I would like to keep her with me."

It was sad to admit, but she needed company tonight. She didn't want to be alone. Even if there was only a baby to fill that role.

Joseph crouched down beside them. "I don't mind missing her three a.m. feeding. You can keep her overnight anytime you wish."

Leah grew excited at the sight of him. He gave her his finger to hold. She immediately pulled it to her mouth. He looked at Anne. "Don't worry. I washed my hands after I milked my goats."

"I should hope so. Why don't you pull up a chair and listen to this story. I think you'll enjoy it."

"Is it about goats?" He pulled a chair over and sat down. He offered his finger to Leah again and she grabbed it.

"It's about a little girl who has lost her puppy. Leah likes it." At least, she liked the pictures.

"She would like it better if it was a story about goats."

Anne struggled not to smile. "When she is at your home, you can read to her from your *Goat World* magazine. When she is here, she is going to learn that there is more to life than goats and milking machines."

"And you think a story about a puppy will do that?"

"This is about a very naughty, adventuresome puppy who learns that home is the best place of all."

"Okay. As long as there is a good moral, I guess she can hear the story even if it doesn't have a goat in it. Start at the beginning. I don't want to miss anything."

Anne smiled and turned back to the first page. She put more animation in her voice as she retold the tale. Several times she caught him chuckling at the story. A month ago she never would have imagined that her neighbor had an adorable sense of humor or that his laugh could make her warm all over.

It was nice having him to keep her company. It was wonderful to see the affection in his eyes as he played peekaboo with Leah while she read. Having him there felt comfortable. It felt right. It felt like they were a family.

They weren't. She knew that. But just for a little while, it was wonderful to pretend they were the family in the book, rejoicing over the return of their missing puppy. Was that so wrong? Or was she setting herself up for heartbreak?

Chapter Fifteen

Dora Stoltzfus stood at Anne's side while she weighed Dora's baby boy at his checkup. He was Dora's first child. She and her husband had been nervous wrecks during the pregnancy, calling Anne out several times on false alarms. Always late at night. But as a new mother, Dora was proving to be a natural. Her husband, Wayne, was a distant cousin of Anne's. It had been his mother who'd written to Anne asking her to consider moving to the area after the community's last midwife passed away.

Dora leaned closer to Anne. "I heard a rumor that you are walking out with Joseph Lapp."

Anne could barely contain her dismay. "Where did you hear such a thing?"

"My mother-in-law was at McCann's Grocery last evening when Alma Miller came in. Alma said you and Joseph were out for a buggy ride yesterday morning and she saw he had his arm around you. In broad daylight. Alma was shocked. It's not as if the two of you are silly teenagers. You are both baptized members of the church. So what's the story?"

Anne decided to stall until she could think of a plausible explanation. "Mrs. Miller got it wrong. Nine pounds and ten ounces. Your son is growing like a weed." She handed the squirming naked baby back to his mother.

"That's because he eats all the time. I'm lucky to get anything done around the house."

"Isn't your husband helping?" Anne was happy to change the subject.

"With housework? Not a chance. His mother is staying with us, though. I don't know what I would do without her. Lovina has been wonderful. When I first married her son, I thought she didn't like me. But she sure likes her grandson. She calls him *Gottes Shenkas*."

God's gift. Anne smiled. The feeling of being close to God was one of the things she loved most about delivering babies. She took a seat at her desk and began writing her notes in Dora's chart. "Babies have a way of bringing people together. They are pure and simple love from our Lord above."

"*Ja*, they are." Dora kissed her son's forehead and began to dress him. "So how did Alma Miller get it wrong? Was Joseph with someone else? Or were you with someone else?" she asked with renewed interest.

Since the truth was generally the best way to go, Anne replied, "Joseph and I were together. My horse came up lame and Joseph offered to drive me to see Rhonda Yoder. That's all. We are not walking out together."

"Then he didn't have his arm around you?"

She closed her eyes and shook her head. Stick to the facts. "Actually, he did, but only because the horse bolted and I was thrown sideways. He saved me from being dumped off the seat."

"Interesting." Dora didn't appear completely convinced. "I thought it was strange because I didn't think you liked him. I thought you were sweet on Micah Shetler."

"I'm not sweet on Micah and I never said I disliked Joseph. I disliked the fact that he wouldn't keep his goats out of my garden. I was ready to complain to the bishop about it."

"Is that why he's putting up a new fence today?"

Anne looked up from her notes. "He is?"

"I saw him unloading a wagon full of mesh wire and T posts when I drove up."

"Really." She rose from her chair, walked through the house and looked out the kitchen window. Sure enough, Joseph was out in his pasture driving T posts into the ground. He had a row of them about ten feet apart along his existing fence. Leah sat in her stroller several yards away from him. A few of his goats were standing around sniffing her. Anne hoped they wouldn't start eating the sweater the babe was wearing. Surely, Joseph would notice that.

"Is it true that his sister just left her baby with him?"

"Sadly, that is true. I have been helping him take care of Leah, and he has been doing chores for me in exchange."

"It makes it easy that the two of you live so close together."

"It does, but it also makes us food for gossips since we are coming and going between the two houses often. I hope you'll set anyone straight who mentions we are walking out."

"I will do that, but it's a shame you aren't seeing him."

"Why do you say that?"

"A baby needs a mother. Joseph should marry if he intends to raise the child. It's not right to let her grow up motherless. I hope he knows that. Has he said anything about taking a wife?"

"*Nay*, he hasn't." She frowned at the idea of another woman taking over Leah's care. Was it something Joseph was considering? He hadn't mentioned it.

"If he doesn't wish to wed, my sister and her husband have been trying to have a baby for seven years. They would adopt that little girl in a heartbeat."

Anne shook her head. "I don't think he would give her up."

"He would if he realized it was best for the *bubbel*. When do you want to see me again?"

"As long as you are feeling good and the baby is doing well, a month from today."

"Sounds fine to me. You were a wonderful labor coach, Anne. You made the whole experience something Wayne and I will always remember and cherish."

"You did all the work, Dora. Don't give me the credit." The two women hugged and Dora left with her son in her arms. Wayne sat in the buggy outside waiting on them. He waved at Anne and helped his wife into the buggy. They settled close together and he touched his son's face lovingly.

After they left, Anne walked across her field to where Joseph was putting up the fence. She hated to tell him what she had heard, but she knew he needed to know. He'd taken his coat off and was working with his shirtsleeves rolled up. His forearms were tanned and muscular. He handled the heavy posts and sledgehammer with ease. Was Dora right? Should he marry to give Leah a mother?

"Wee gayt's," he called out as she drew near.

"Good day. I see you have been busy since you picked Leah up this morning. Why didn't you leave her with me?"

He glanced at the baby trying to grab the closest goat. "I was missing my girl. She's not been a bit of trouble. In fact, she put in the first six posts for me."

The image of a baby driving a six-foot steel

post into the ground made Anne giggle. "That explains why they're crooked."

He turned to look down the line. "They aren't crooked."

"And they weren't put in by a baby, either. I can't believe you are doing this."

"It was time."

She almost said "Past time," but she held her tongue. "Dora Stoltzfus told me something I thought you'd want to hear."

"Oh? What was that?"

"Alma Miller has been telling people that we are walking out together."

"How would Alma Miller know such a thing?"

"She saw us riding together in the buggy."

"That's not a crime."

"You had your arm around me in broad daylight, which seems to be a crime in Alma's book."

Joseph came to stand opposite Anne at the fence. "I hope you set Dora straight."

"I did. I explained the circumstances, and I told her there was nothing between us. I'm taking care of Leah and that's all there is."

She waited to see his reaction because a part of her was beginning to hope that what she said wasn't true. There was an attraction growing between them. At least on her part. Did he feel the same way?

Joseph cringed inwardly. Anne spoke so adamantly when she insisted there was nothing personal to their relationship. When he heard her put it so strongly, the words hurt. Maybe there wasn't for her, but there was for him. He had started to care about Anne. How did he tell her that when she was trying to convince others of the exact opposite?

"I'd like to believe we are friends, you and I," he ventured, waiting to see her reaction.

She plucked at a weed that had grown through the fence. "Of course we're friends, but I'm not sure others will understand that."

At least that was something. Her friendship was better than nothing, but he realized it wasn't enough. Maybe in time she would come to think of him as more than a friend.

Was he foolish to hope her feelings would change? The only thing he could do was continue to offer his friendship. And that meant getting the rest of the posts in. "I should get back to work."

Anne remained at the fence. He could see she wanted to say something else. "Is there more?"

"More talk about us? Not that I know of. I need to ask you a favor, but in light of what I just told you, I'm not sure if I should."

"I can't say yes or no until I hear the question."

"I'm out of several of the ingredients I need to make Leah's formula. Daisy is still limping and I can't drive her to town. Is there any chance you could drive me? I see that you're busy. If you can't, that's okay. I think I can handle Duncan if you will allow me to borrow him, but Leah has to stay with you."

He brightened at the chance to do something else for her. "You can't take my horse. I would feel awful if something happened to you and I had to find a new nanny for Leah."

He was rewarded with a tiny smile from her. "Only because you would have to find a new nanny?"

He rolled down his sleeves and pulled on his coat. "Should I have another reason?"

"Because you wouldn't want to cause your friend pain and suffering?"

He moved to stand in front of her. Softly, he

said, "That's true. I would never want to hurt you, Anne."

Her cheeks grew pink. "*Danki*. I would never knowingly hurt you, either. That's why I wasn't sure I should ask you to take me to town. What if there is more talk about us?"

"People will always talk. Leah needs her formula. Come to think of it, I need to pick up a few things, too. Shall we go to McCann's Grocery or Miller's General Store?"

He began pushing Leah's stroller toward the gate. Anne walked along on her side of the fence. "McCann's should have everything I need. What about you?"

"Miller's. I need some small-gauge wire to fasten the fence to these posts. I don't have enough on hand. We need to stop at the Beachy Craft Shop after that."

"Why?"

"It's a gathering place. We need to put out the word that you require the loan of a buggy horse until Daisy gets better so I don't have to keep driving you places."

Her expression fell. "I'm sorry it's an inconvenience."

He stopped to face her. "It's not. But if others believe that to be true, our being seen together won't be so remarked upon, and you will soon have a drivable horse."

"That's a good idea."

"Don't sound so surprised. I have them once in a while." He started walking again. When they reached the gate, he opened it and pushed the stroller over to her side.

Anne looked the gate over with a puzzled expression. She swung it back and forth. "Did you fix my gate?"

"How come it is my poor fence, but it's your fixed gate?"

She rolled her eyes. "Very well. Did you fix *your* gate?"

"I did, and I added a weight to it so that it will close on its own and swing in either direction."

"You have been ambitious today."

He enjoyed the admiration in her tone. He started making a mental list of other projects that might please her. "I'll be back with the buggy in a few minutes."

"Leah and I will be ready."

The ride into Honeysuckle didn't take long. They stopped at McCann's Grocery first because it was closest. Anne got out. Joseph stayed put. "Aren't you coming in?"

"I thought I would sit here looking annoyed and bored."

She giggled. "In other words, normal for you."

He started to smile but quickly smothered it. "I don't want it to look like we are enjoying each other's company. Now hurry up. And you're right, annoyed and bored is normal for me."

Anne chose to take Leah with her. Inside the store, she set the infant carrier inside one of the shopping carts and started down the closest aisle. It didn't take her long to find what she needed, but it did take her a while to get out of the store. She ran into three different women she knew and had to explain to each one of them who Leah was.

By the time she got out, she thought Joseph would truly be annoyed with her for keeping him waiting so long. To her surprise, he was busy talking to the husbands of the women she had encountered. Five men were gathered around one of the buggy horses. Joseph caught sight of her and beckoned her over.

"What do you think of this mare?" The horse was a sturdy-looking black-and-white pinto.

Anne looked her over carefully. "She's a very pretty animal."

"Her disposition is just as sweet," Calvin Miller said. His wife, Alma, was the one who had been spreading gossip about Anne and Joseph.

"Would you be willing to rent her to me for a week or two?" Anne asked.

"I'll loan her to you for a week. No rent needed. Joseph was just telling us how his old goat lamed your mare."

"She hates that goat," Joseph added dryly.

"Because he's a menace and you won't keep him locked up," she snapped, rounding on him.

Joseph folded his arms and scowled. "I was putting up a new fence when you decided you needed to come to town today. Don't complain if he's in your garden tomorrow because I didn't get it done."

A couple of the men snickered but quieted when Anne shot them a sharp look. She turned to Calvin. "I would deeply appreciate the loan of your mare. Can you bring her by soon? I would hate to tear Joseph away from his fence building if I need to deliver a baby again. Although I am grateful he found the time to take me out to see Rhonda Yoder yesterday."

Calvin stroked his long beard. "I heard it was a near thing with her babe. The little fellow had a cord around his neck three times. It was *Gottes* mercy that saved him."

All the men nodded and murmured in agreement. How did he and his wife gather so much information in such a short period of time? It was truly amazing.

Calvin patted the mare's neck. "I'll bring Pocahontas along to the church service tomorrow and you can take her home from there."

"That would be *wunderbar*."

Joseph unfolded his arms. "*Goot*. Can we go now? I need to pick up that wire at Miller's General Store before they close."

"I'm ready when you are," she said with a stiff smile.

They walked away from the group and Joseph helped her up into his buggy. He whispered, "How was that?"

"You almost convinced me we don't like each other."

"Then we should confound them even further. It is getting late. How would you like to have dinner with me at the Mennonite Family Restaurant?"

"What reason will we give for going there?"

He rubbed his stomach. "Anne, I'm hungry. I haven't had lunch or dinner today. I've been putting up fence and running you all over town."

"Oh, in that case, *danki*. I'll be happy to join you. They have a very nice buffet on Saturdays."

"Sounds perfect."

Anne waited in the buggy with Leah while Joseph purchased his wire. He was out of the store in record time. They left the buggy where it was and walked to the restaurant. It was busy inside, but the waitress was able to seat them at a small booth in the back corner and brought them two large glasses of sweet iced tea.

Most of the patrons were Amish families enjoying a special night out. A few were *Englisch* folk, tourists, from the way they gawked at those in Plain dress. The room was cozy with green-and-white-checked tablecloths and curtains on the windows. The benches in the booths were covered in solid green vinyl to match them.

Joseph stayed with Leah while Anne filled

her plate. When she came back, she sat down and waited for him to return. He came back with two heaping plates of food.

Anne looked at him in amazement. "Can you really eat all that?"

"This will be a good start. Did you see the dessert bar? I'm hankering for a big piece of that carrot cake."

"Poor Margaret." Anne shook her head.

He began to salt his mound of potatoes. "Who's Margaret?"

"She's the owner of this place and she's going to lose money on you."

He gestured toward Anne's plate. "*Nay*, she won't. You eat like a bird. We will balance each other."

Anne coveted the warmth spilling through her veins. They did balance each other in many ways. She dropped her gaze to her hands folded on the table. Was she being foolish to believe it could lead to something more?

What did the soft expression on Anne's face mean? Joseph knew she wasn't indifferent to him. If she liked him, maybe she cared more than she let on.

Leah kicked and cooed in her basket. Anne picked her up, but Joseph said, "I'll take her."

He settled her on his lap, took the baby's hands and held them between his own as he bowed his head to pray. Leah protested only briefly before keeping still. Joseph began silently reciting the *Gebet Nach Dem Essen*, the Prayer Before Meals.

O Lord God, heavenly Father, bless us and these Thy gifts, which we accept from Thy tender goodness. Give us food and drink also for our souls unto life eternal, that we may share at Thy heavenly table, through Jesus Christ. Amen.

He followed it with the Lord's Prayer, also prayed silently, knowing he had much to be thankful for but still asking God to bring Fannie home soon.

Joseph lifted his head, signaling the end of the prayer for Anne. He patted Leah's cheek and told her what a good girl she was. Anne looked pleased with both of them as she took Leah from him and settled the baby on her shoulder.

The smell of baking bread and pot roast filled the air. Joseph thought back to the food his mother used to make. Roast beef and roast pork, fried chicken and potatoes, schnitzel with sauerkraut, all served piping hot from her stove with fresh bread smeared with butter and vegetables from her garden. He hadn't given a thought to how much work his mother had done without complaint until she was gone.

Cooking was a struggle after that. Fannie eventually grew up and learned enough to take over the kitchen, but she never found the joy in it his mother seemed to have. Maybe it was because his mother had a husband she wished to please and *kinner* to watch grow big and strong on the meals she gave them.

Anne would be like that. He could see her making sure all her children ate their vegetables and drank their milk. She should have little ones.

To do that, she would have to marry.

"Anne, I'm surprised to see you here."

Joseph looked over his shoulder to see Micah Shetler approaching with a friendly grin on his handsome face. Joseph's enjoyment of the evening started going downhill.

Chapter Sixteen

Anne was pleasantly surprised to see Micah Shetler approaching. She had wondered how he was doing now that his brother was about to marry the woman Micah had been courting only a few weeks ago.

"*Wee gayt's*, Micah. How have you been?"

"Busy."

"I'm sure you are with your brother's wedding approaching." She gave him a sympathetic smile. Both Micah and his brother, Neziah, had been walking out with her friend Ellen Beachy. Their father and Ellen's father had decided it was time Ellen married and she was expected to choose one of the brothers. At first it had looked as though Micah would be her husband, but then Neziah had won her heart. She'd fallen in love with him and they would marry in a few days.

If Micah was suffering from a broken heart, it didn't show, although there was something different about him now. She couldn't put her finger on what it was.

"I drove by the other day and saw your stand was closed for the season. I stopped in but you weren't home."

"I'm sorry I missed you."

He gestured toward Leah. "Are you keeping the babies that you deliver now?"

"*Nay*, this is Joseph's niece."

"Anne is acting as her nanny until her mother returns." Joseph's annoyed tone made Anne glance at him sharply. Why was he upset?

Micah noticed, too, but it seemed to amuse him. "You couldn't find a more caring and capable woman than Anne to look after the child. I would let her take care of all my *kinner*. Of course, I don't have any. But who knows? That may change one day."

"One day soon?" Anne teased.

"You'll be among the first to know. It was good seeing you, Anne. I may stop in again one of these days."

"I'm always happy to see you." She wondered with dismay if he was going to ask her to walk out with him. He was a fine, good-looking man, but she wasn't on the hunt for a husband. Why else would he want to speak to her?

He walked away and stopped at another table where a young Amish woman sat with her parents. Anne didn't recognize them. They weren't from her church district. She noticed the way the girl pointedly avoided looking at Micah as he spoke to her father. What surprised Anne was the warm way Micah's glance rested on the young woman. Was there a new romance blooming in his life?

"Joseph, do you know the family Micah is speaking with?"

"Henry Hochstetler. He owns a harness shop over in the next town. He's done some work for me."

"Is that his wife and daughter?"

"*Ja.* Why do you ask?"

"No real reason."

"Micah is a friend of yours?"

She glanced at Joseph and found him watching her intently. "I guess you could say that. He's always been nice to me."

"He's nice to all the women." Joseph stabbed his slice of meat loaf with his fork.

"True," she admitted. Micah was known as something of a flirt, but the same could be said for his father, Simeon Shetler. Anne knew neither of them meant any harm. As Micah walked away from Henry Hochstetler and his family, the daughter finally looked up. When she did, her eyes followed Micah with poignant longing.

"Why would he be coming to visit you?" Joseph asked.

"I have no idea. His brother is marrying my friend, so perhaps it has something to do with the wedding plans."

"That's not likely."

"Is there a reason you dislike Micah?" she asked, intrigued by the hostility she sensed.

"I never said that."

"Sounds that way to me."

"You're wrong. I've nothing against the man."

"I'm sorry I misunderstood." She wasn't wrong. He did dislike Micah. She decided to change the subject. "How's that meat loaf? I might get a piece."

"It's *goot*. How's your salad?"

"It's okay, but I don't care for the dressing."

"Try the pickled okra. It's great."

"Yuck."

"You don't like okra?" He looked stunned.

She shook her head. "Not pickled. Fried is okay, but not pickled. I don't care for pickled anything."

"Pickled beets?"

"Nope."

"Sauerkraut? Everyone likes sauerkraut."

"Not everyone. What food do you dislike?"

He shrugged. "I don't know. I haven't tasted it yet."

"When you marry, your wife is going to find you very easy to cook for."

"What makes you think I'm going to marry?"

"I just assumed you would when you met the right woman."

He grew somber. "I did meet her. A long time ago."

"I'm sorry. I heard about your loss." He didn't mention her name. The Amish rarely spoke about those who had passed away.

"It was *Gottes* will," he said.

"All is the will of God," Anne agreed, think-

ing of the baby whose name she never spoke
aloud but would carry in her heart forever.

What would Joseph say if he learned her
story? Would he be forgiving? Or would he decide to find another woman to look after Leah?
One without a blemished past. No one in Honeysuckle knew about her unwed pregnancy.
That secret had remained in Ohio, known only
to a few members of her family.

Joseph would never learn about that part of
her life unless she decided to share it with him
and she had no reason to do so.

The following day was Church Sunday,
which was held at the home of an Amish family who lived less than two miles from Anne.
Her mare, Daisy, was still limping, but Anne
was able to walk the distance easily. She
would've walked much farther to avoid riding to the prayer meeting with Joseph. That
would really set tongues wagging.

Joseph arrived with Leah a short time after
Anne reached the farmhouse. His arrival gen-
erated a number of comments from the women
who were bringing food into the home and preparing to feed the congregation later. When
questioned, Anne assured those who would

listen that she was not romantically involved with Joseph. Some of her friends winked and smiled as if they didn't believe her. She wasn't surprised that she had to defend herself, but she was surprised by the number of older women who voiced their concerns about Leah being raised without a mother. By a man who wasn't her father. That Joseph was her uncle seem to carry little weight with them.

From her place among the unmarried women during the service, Anne could see Joseph and Leah from the corner of her eye. She didn't dare turn her attention to him. Halfway through the three-hour-long prayer meeting, Leah's patience evaporated and she began to fuss. Joseph took her outside. Anne followed as unobtrusively as she could. She found them at the rear of his buggy. "Do you want me to take her for a while?"

"She needs to be changed and fed. I can manage."

"I know you can. But now that I have come outside, it might be best if I returned in the role of a nanny."

"I reckon you're right. Has there been more talk?"

"Not about us so much." She wasn't sure

how to broach the subject the women had been discussing.

"About Fannie?" He looked braced to hear the worst.

"*Nay*, it's nothing. Idle chatter. Go back and I'll bring Leah in when she is finished with her bottle. I'll keep her with me until after the preaching is done." Maybe if the women saw Leah was getting adequate attention from Anne, they would be less critical of Joseph. She wasn't Leah's mother, but she would do her best to provide the child with a role model.

She kept the baby with her for the rest of the morning. Once the service was over, she carried Leah outside, happy to show off the good-natured baby to those who admired her.

It wasn't long before Joseph approached. "I'm leaving now."

"You don't intend to stay for the meal?" she asked, wishing he would make an effort to join in with the community.

"I have two sick goats I need to tend. I'll take Calvin Miller's horse home for you."

Anne handed over Leah, and he left without another word. She glanced at the women around her and saw disapproval on several faces. Joseph needed to realize he wasn't alone.

He was part of a large and caring community. All he had to do was reach out to them to be accepted. The more he distanced himself, the less they were able to know and understand him.

"He would be a good match for you, Anne," Rhonda whispered in her ear. She and her husband had chosen to attend services with Anne's church since they were staying with Naomi until Rhonda's mother arrived to help the young couple with their newborn son.

"I'm not looking for a match."

"I wasn't either when I found Silas. Now look at us."

Dora joined their group. "I agree. The babe needs a mother. You should marry him."

"I can hardly marry a man who hasn't proposed to me." Anne reined in her irritation.

"I think Micah has his eye on you," Rebecca Yoder added. She was Rhonda's sister-in-law and still single. She glanced across the way to where the young men were gathered in groups.

Anne shook her head. "Micah can put his eyes back in his head. I'm not going to marry anyone!"

She left the group to visit with Naomi for a while, then headed home. She was happy to have the long walk alone with her thoughts.

* * *

Joseph was working on his last section of fence posts when he saw Micah drive up to Anne's home on Monday morning. Joseph didn't pause in his work. He knew Anne was gone. She had been called out two hours ago to attend a delivery. He had Leah in the stroller at his side as he worked.

"Good day, Joseph," Micah called cheerfully as he approached after he realized Anne wasn't home.

"Good enough, I guess." Joseph drove in the last stake.

"Do you happen to know where Anne is?"

"Gone to deliver a baby."

"So there is no telling when she will be back?"

"Nope."

Micah looked disappointed. "I guess I can stick around for a while in case she comes back soon. Would you like some help?"

"The stakes are all in."

"I can help stretch the wire. It's a two-man job."

It was easier with two. Joseph shrugged. "Suit yourself."

Micah came into the pen and waded through the goats to Joseph's side. "Friendly bunch, aren't they?"

"I think so." Joseph pulled a roll of wire off his wagon and began unrolling it.

Micah grabbed the loose end and pulled it to the corner post. "Do you mind if I ask you a question about Anne?"

"What about her?" Joseph fastened the fencing to the post with small strips of wire that he tightened with a pair of pliers.

"There's some talk going around that you are walking out with her. I was wondering if that's true."

"What difference does it make to you?"

"If you aren't seeing Anne, then I'd like to ask her to walk out with me."

"She is my niece's nanny. That's all. She watches the baby while I work and I help her with her garden and fix things around the farm."

"That's good to know. I didn't want to step on anyone's toes."

They finished stretching the fence and securing it by early afternoon. Joseph was grateful for the help, but he was happier when Micah finally gave up and left without seeing Anne.

Would she walk out with him? There was no reason she shouldn't. Micah was a well-liked member of the community. Joseph had no reason to dislike the man, but he did.

And in a moment of honesty, he realized it was because Micah was interested in Anne. Not as a nanny or as a midwife but as a woman and a potential wife.

Why did the thought of Micah and Anne together irritate him so? Joseph never imagined himself as the dog in a manger, but apparently, he was. He wasn't interested in her as a wife. He enjoyed her friendship. He liked her smile. He wanted to see her happy.

He took the handles of Leah's stroller and began pushing her toward his house. Just because he was happy being single, didn't mean Anne was happy being single. Women were different. They wanted different things in life. If she wanted Micah, then he would be happy for her.

Maybe.

Matilda came to his side. The rest of the herd followed along. She looked up at him with wise brown eyes. Joseph had to admit the truth. "Maybe I wouldn't be happy about it."

It didn't seem right. He couldn't imagine Anne and Micah as a couple. Being married. Matilda bleated softly.

Joseph nodded. "*Ja*, I know. They don't fit together."

The more he thought about it, the more upset he became. Anne would be a wonderful mother and wife, but she deserved someone who loved her. Not someone who decided to take a wife because his brother was marrying the woman he truly wanted. Anne wasn't second best. She deserved better.

Matilda paused to scratch her ankle with her nose. He paused and looked down at her. "I know. It's none of my business what she wants."

"What who wants?"

His gaze shot from Matilda to the new gate, where Anne stood waiting for his reply. "Nothing."

"Joseph, were you talking to the goat?"

"I was. What of it?"

Anne's eyebrow rose a fraction. "Did she answer you?"

"*Nay*, she was no help at all."

Anne pushed open the gate. "That's a relief. *Hallo*, Leah. Are you ready to come to my house while your *onkel* gets the milking done?"

He pushed the stroller out of his pen and up to Anne. "Micah dropped by to see you."

"He said he might." She began walking toward her house.

Joseph glanced at her as he fell into step beside her. She didn't look particularly excited by the news. "He waited for several hours."

"That's too bad. Did you tell him what I was doing?"

"I did. He wanted to wait, anyway. He helped me finish my fence. We spent a lot of time talking."

"I noticed you had the fence up. Alvin and Mary King had a healthy baby girl."

She didn't act like a woman smitten with a fellow. Joseph stopped walking. "That's good to hear. Don't you want to know what Micah and I talked about?"

She kept walking. "Not really."

"We talked about you."

"That wouldn't take up several hours."

"You underestimate your attraction, Anne."

She rounded on him. "What are you talking about?"

"Micah is interested in walking out with you."

She planted her hands on her hips. "Did he ask you to be his go-between?"

Chapter Seventeen

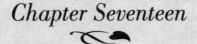

Anne knew it was common practice for a young Amish man to have a member of the girl's family or one of her friends find out if she would be receptive to his courting. She considered it something bashful teenage boys engaged in. Not grown men.

Joseph stared at his feet. "Not exactly."

"Then what *exactly* did he say?"

"He wanted to know if you and I were walking out."

"I'm getting very tired of answering that question. I hope you set him straight."

Joseph held up both hands. "I told him you were Leah's nanny. Nothing else."

That didn't exactly flatter her. "*Goot.* What else did he say?"

"I reckon I should let him tell you."

She closed her eyes. "I knew it. He wants to ask me out again, doesn't he?"

"You don't sound very happy about it."

"I'm *not* happy about it. I'm not interested in walking out with Micah. He's a nice man, but he isn't the one for me."

Joseph sighed in relief. "I'm glad to hear you say that."

"What does that mean?"

He looked taken aback. "Just that he doesn't seem right for you."

She planted her hands on her hips again. "Since when do you get to decide who is the right man for me?"

He dropped his gaze to his boots. "That's not what I meant."

She took Leah's stroller from him. "I am in charge of my own life. If I wish to walk out with Micah, I will do that."

"I only said that he didn't seem right for you. You are free to choose. You would make any man a fine wife."

He looked so contrite that she began to feel she had overreacted. "I'm sorry. It's not you. My friends are all telling me who to go out with and who I should wed. No one is asking me what I want."

"What do you want, Anne?" he asked quietly.

Anne met his gaze. There was genuine concern in his beautiful stormy-gray eyes.

She bent to unbuckle Leah from her stroller and lifted the babe to her shoulders. "I don't know."

That was a lie. She did know. She wanted the man with the stormy eyes to want her. Not as a nanny, a friend, a neighbor, but as a man wants a woman he has come to cherish. It was a foolish thought, but it had taken root in her heart and she couldn't weed it out. Her head said it wasn't possible but her heart wasn't ready to give up.

He stepped close and placed a hand on Anne's shoulder. "When you do know, I hope God grants you all that you desire."

How was that to happen when Joseph was blind to anything but her friendship?

The next few days passed in a comfortable pattern for Joseph. He rose early, got Leah up and dressed her for the day. He carried her to Anne's house, had a cup of coffee with her, then did his milking and chores. He took care of his horse, fed and watered Anne's horses, cleaned the stalls and made sure the animals were all in good health. Daisy's leg improved, but he knew it was time for her to retire from pulling a buggy. Anne would have to buy a new horse soon.

In the late morning, Anne would bring Leah to his place when he was done working outside. Leah stayed with him until the evening milking, when Anne came to pick her up again.

After he was finished, he walked the hundred yards to Anne's house again. On Wednesday night he found her in a flurry of activity.

"What's the occasion?" he asked, noting the array of baked goods on the counter.

"The wedding," she said happily.

He frowned. "What wedding?"

"Ellen Beachy and Neziah Shetler."

"I forgot all about it. Are you going?"

She glanced over her shoulder. "Of course I'm going. Aren't you?"

"I hadn't thought about it."

"You got an invitation, didn't you?"

"I don't usually go to these things."

She stopped stirring something on the stove and turned to face him. "You should start."

"Why?"

"Because people need to see that you are raising Leah according to our ways."

"I take her to church."

"Our community is much more than a church service. It's about fellowship and friendship. It's about being able to depend on each other. Almost from the time an Amish child is born, they know where they belong, that they are loved and cherished. By everyone, not just their families. Leah needs to be a part of that. She needs to form bonds and friendships."

"She will when she goes to school." He picked her up from her playpen.

"She won't feel that she belongs if you don't feel that way, Joseph."

He wouldn't look at Anne. "You will take her to the weddings and picnics and haystack suppers. She will learn what she needs from you."

Anne sighed heavily. "I'm a temporary nanny. I'm not her parent."

"Neither am I. I didn't want this responsibility. I didn't ask for it. Why is it up to me?" He took Leah and left, letting the door slam behind him.

Regretting his outburst the minute he stepped outside, Joseph walked toward home with lagging steps. He hadn't gone far when he heard her voice behind him.

"Joseph, wait."

He stopped. "I wasn't cut out to be a parent. I know it. You don't need to point it out."

"I wasn't trying to do that."

"All I want is to be left alone and to raise my goats. Why can't I do that?"

"Because you belong among us. You are part of the whole that is the fabric of this place and our people."

"Am I? Maybe Fannie had the right idea. Leave and have done with it. Why pretend to be something I'm not?"

Anne laid a hand on his arm. "You don't believe that."

"I'm not sure what I believe anymore."

He expected more arguments from her, but she simply said, "All right. I'll take Leah to the wedding with me if you will permit it. You don't have to come."

It was what he wanted, wasn't it? *"Danki.* I'll have her ready."

As Anne walked away, Joseph knew he had failed some test in her eyes. He went home, but he slept fitfully that night. When morning came, he had Leah ready before Anne drove up in her buggy. He walked out on the porch with the baby asleep in her basket.

He handed Leah up to Anne. "She had a bottle a half hour ago."

"Okay. I'll be home before dark."

"Enjoy yourself."

"I will. You can come later if you feel like it. For the dinner or for the supper. You'll be welcome."

"I doubt I'll make it."

She nodded but didn't speak. Picking up the reins, she turned the spotted mare around and drove away.

As he watched them go, a bitter sense of loss settled in his chest. He had gotten his wish. He was alone and it wasn't what he wanted, after all. The only person he had to blame was himself.

Anne put another dozen plates in the dishwater and added a small squirt of soap to the waning suds in the tub set up on a sawhorse at the side of the house. As a friend of the bride, she was doing her part to help Ellen's family during the massive undertaking. The wedding had gone off beautifully and the dinner was winding down. Anne had no idea how many people had been fed, but she guessed it was over two hundred. She began scrubbing the plates. Once the dinner was done, the preparations for the evening meal would get under way. Amish weddings were an all-day affair.

She glanced beside her. Leah was finally asleep again in her Moses basket. She had been held and passed around by the older girls responsible for watching the younger *kinner* for most of the morning. As far as Anne could tell, Leah had enjoyed every minute of the attention.

She heard a buggy rolling in and washed faster. They would need the plates to feed the newcomers. Glancing in the direction of the sound, she let a dish slip back into the soapy water. Joseph stepped out of his buggy looking very handsome in his dark Sunday suit and black hat. His suit fit snuggly over his broad shoulders. The dark material made his gray eyes look brighter. He pulled his hat off and smoothed his thick blond hair with one hand. He wasn't smiling, but Anne's heart skipped with happiness at the sight of his dear, sweet face. She knew how hard this was for him, but he was making the effort for Leah.

After handing his horse over to the young

man parking the buggies, he walked toward the house. He stopped when he saw Anne. He gave her a brief nod and walked inside.

She was so happy for him that she wanted to sing for joy. It was a start. If he wanted, he could find his way back into the tight-knit community and he wouldn't have to be alone. And best of all, Leah wouldn't grow up in his self-imposed isolation, as Anne feared she might.

Anne didn't mention his attendance at the wedding when Joseph saw her the next day, but he knew she was pleased with him. She was smiling and happy, singing as she worked in the house. He took his time finishing his coffee. He liked the sound of her voice floating down the stairs as she stripped the sheets to wash them. It was hard to leave and get his own work done but he finally tore himself away. She brought him lunch when she brought Leah back after the morning milking. Thick slices of ham and cheese on homemade bread. It was a rare treat for him.

That evening, he wondered if she would bring supper, too, but she showed up on his doorstep with only Leah.

"I decided that it's time," she said brightly.

A half smile tugged at his lips. "Time for what?"

"To prove my friendship, and because I agreed to it as a way to repay you for getting my pumpkins sold, I will do the milking this evening."

He clapped a hand to his chest. "Be still, my happy heart. Are you serious?"

She handed him the baby. She was wide-awake. He held her to his shoulder. Anne started walking toward the barn. "The house is clean. Supper is in the oven. I find I have some free time this evening. You will have to watch Leah."

"I think I may need to sit down. I never thought I would see this day."

"You already know I can do this. You showed me how. I'm reasonably sure I remember everything you told me." She pulled open the barn door.

"On second thought, I won't sit down. I'm coming with you."

"That sounds like you don't trust me." She shot him a saucy grin.

"I absolutely trust you but this is some very expensive equipment."

She flipped on a switch. He heard the generators start up. A few seconds later, the lights came on. She smiled. "So far, so good. This isn't hard at all."

Joseph gave a bark of laughter. She raised her chin and walked to the door that opened to the goats' pen. "Here, girls. Up you go!"

The goats came in and they kept coming. She tried to close the door but they squeezed past her. Those in the lead ran to their stanchions. Those that didn't have a place began crowding the others out of the way. Several of them fell off the platform and tried crawling underneath to get at the feed in the wheelbarrow on the other side. Anne struggled desperately to get the door closed, but another goat got her head through and Anne couldn't latch it. "Joseph, help me!"

"You're right. It's not hard at all. You are doing fine."

Anne could have cheerfully chucked another tomato at him. Maybe even a pumpkin. Why did he have to be enjoying himself at her expense? "What do I do?"

Chuckling, he walked to her side. He put his

hand on the goat's nose and pushed her back. "Wait your turn, Abigail."

The goat backed out, and Anne was finally able to shut the door. She looked at the mass of goats milling about inside. "Now what?"

He pointed to the ramp leading down from the milking platform. "Open the out door."

Anne made her way through the herd and opened the door he indicated. The goats reluctantly began to leave. They expected to be milked and fed and they were confused. Joseph hurried them along with slaps on their rear ends. After a few minutes, the area was clear.

"Do you want to try this again?" He was struggling not to laugh as he balanced Leah on his shoulder.

Anne shuddered. "Not particularly, but how else am I going to learn?"

"*Goot* girl. Open the in door only wide enough for one goat at a time. Count them as they come through. We can only milk twelve. Shut the door on the thirteenth goat. If she gets her head in, a thump on the nose will make her back out."

Anne gathered her resolve and returned to the door. She slid it open a little way, using her knee to keep it from being fully opened by the rush. When she had twelve, she pushed the door shut. Just like last time, one more goat got her head in. Anne pushed her back. "Wait your turn, Abigail."

"That is Jenny," Joseph said.

"I don't care what her name is—I want her to get back!" The goat complied and Anne slid the door closed. She dusted her hands off, feeling pleased with her effort.

That soon faded. It took her four hours to finish milking. It normally took Joseph just under two. When the last goat went out the door, he showed Anne how to clean the milkers and tubing and then said, "You're done."

Her *kapp* had come off in her struggles at the door and hung by a single bobby pin from the back of her bun. Her feet were bruised from the multitude of hooves walking over them and her arms ached from reaching above her head to clean udders and attach milkers. The platform that was waist-high on Joseph was shoulder level for her. She leaned against the metal barn wall. "I'll never do this again."

Joseph came up and put his arm around her, gave her a hug and kissed her forehead. "You did great for your first time."

She was so flabbergasted by his display of

affection that she simply stood there with her mouth open while he walked out.

If goat wrestling got her this much attention, she would definitely do it again.

Chapter Eighteen

The next morning started out as well as the previous day. Anne seemed happy, if a bit stiff after her milking ordeal. Leah was happy, too, after sleeping through the entire night for the first time. Smiles, laughs, gurgles and coos greeted Joseph when he picked her up in the morning. She quickly grabbed a handful of his hair and tried to put it in her mouth. Joseph liked the direction his life was taking. Thanks to Anne, it was all working out.

In the early afternoon, he picked up the mail before loading the last of his yearlings to take to market. He found the usual assortment of junk mail and a single letter that made his heart freeze for an instant before it began hammering wildly.

It was from Fannie, but there was no return address. He tore it open.

Dear Joe,

I'm writing because I know you have been waiting for this letter. I know you, Joe. You think I will change my mind and return to your little goat farm, but I won't. I wised up and left Johnny. He wasn't much of a boyfriend and he certainly wasn't father material. I have to get my life straightened out. I'm in some trouble, but it's nothing you can fix. I have to do this myself. I can't have Leah with me, as much as I want to hold her again. I hope you'll tell her that her mother loves her. I know it doesn't seem that way, but it's true. The best life I can give her is a life with you. I didn't know what a good thing I had when I lived in Honeysuckle until it was too late.

None of this is your fault. Don't blame yourself. I made my own choices and now I have to live with them. Maybe that means I've finally grown up. This is my last letter, brother. Don't look for another

one from me. I will only disappoint you again.
Your baby sister always,
Fannie

Joseph crushed the single page into a tiny ball as grief gripped his heart. She was wrong. It *was* his fault. He had failed her somehow. He hadn't given her what she'd needed.

Smoothing out the letter, he carried it to the house, where he went to his family Bible. It sat in a place of honor on an ornately carved stand that had been made by his great-great-grandfather. He opened the book and leafed through it until he found the story of Moses. Tucking the letter between the pages, he closed the book. Someday he would let Leah read her mother's letter. It might help her understand why her mother had left her. He prayed it would comfort her. It didn't comfort him.

He walked outside and saw he had a visitor. Bishop Andy stepped down from his buggy.

"*Wee gayt's*, Joseph. How are you this cold morning?"

"I'm fine, Bishop. What brings you out this way?" It was unusual for the spiritual leader of the congregation to come calling. Unease settled between Joseph's shoulder blades.

"It has been a while since I've spoken to you. You didn't stay long after the last service. I thought I would see how you are doing."

"I'm fine."

"How is your niece? I understand she was sick."

"Leah is fine now that she's drinking goat's milk. She is with Anne until I finish my chores."

"I won't keep you from your work. Is it true that your sister does not plan to return for the child?"

He couldn't pretend anymore that Fannie would be back. "That is what she said in the last letter I had from her."

"You are a good man, Joseph. Not friendly with your neighbors but always willing to help when there is a need."

"I hope that I do my part."

"And I must do my part for the spiritual health of the congregation God has entrusted to me. Raising a child is a sacred duty. I find myself in an unhappy position, Joseph."

"How so?" He didn't like where this was heading.

"Several members of our community have

expressed concern about your niece. They feel it is not right for a bachelor to rear an infant alone. I am in agreement. A baby needs a mother's touch, a mother's love."

"I would gladly return her to her mother if I knew where she was," he said dryly.

"I'm sure that is true. It is a sad thing for a man to lose his sister to the outside world. My worry is about your niece."

"Anne is taking good care of Leah. She is a kind woman, and she loves the child."

"But is it enough? Is the care of a nanny a substitute for a mother? *Nay*, it is not. I am here to urge you to wed, Joseph. Take a wife and give this baby a mother."

"I don't want a wife. I don't need a wife. I can manage on my own. I raised Fannie by myself."

"She was not an infant at the time your parents died. She had known a mother's love and care. It might have been better had you taken a wife, for it is clear Fannie has wandered far from our teachings. Some will lay that at your door and say it is proof that this babe is better off in a home with both a mother and a father."

Wasn't that what he believed, too? That his

failure had led to his sister falling away from their faith.

"If you cannot in good conscience marry one of the suitable women in our community, I urge you to consider allowing one of our childless couples to raise Leah."

"And if I refuse?"

"This is a very serious matter. I have prayed on it, and I believe I'm only asking what is best for the child. You must pray on it, as well. We will talk again in a few days. It is my fervent hope that you will have reached a decision by then. I don't want to take the child away from you, but I will do what I must."

When the bishop had left, Joseph sank onto his porch steps and put his head in his hands. "What do You want from me, Lord? What do You want? Do You want someone else to raise her? Why leave her with me in the first place and let me grow to love her?"

He couldn't give Leah up. He couldn't. She was more than his only connection to Fannie. She was the child he was learning to love as a father would love a daughter. That left him only one option. Find a wife.

The list of women he would consider was short. There was only one name on it.

Joseph rose to his feet, settled his hat on his head and walked toward Anne's place. She might not know it, but she held the answer to Leah's future. He had to make her understand that. He didn't try fooling himself. It wasn't going to be easy. Anne was set in her ways just as he was, but she loved Leah. That was the key. She loved the child. He saw it every time they were together.

Somehow he had to convince her that they belonged together permanently.

Anne was surprised to see Joseph so early in the day. "I thought you were taking some of the young bucks to the livestock sale in town."

"I've changed my mind. I'll go next week. There is always another sale."

"True. Would you like some coffee? I'm afraid it's getting old. I made it early this morning."

"*Nay*, I'm fine. Where is Leah?"

"She's sleeping in my office. I thought I would get these jars washed so I can start making pumpkin puree." She gestured toward the assortment of gourds lined up along the wall.

"I'm a little tired of the pumpkins decorating my kitchen."

"You are always finding something to do."

"That's because my work never ends." She plunged her hands into the hot soapy water in her sink and began washing her small canning jars and lids.

"There is something I need to talk to you about."

"And what is that? Has Chester eaten my windmill or my buggy?"

"Anne, we've gotten along well together these last few weeks. Don't you think?"

She chuckled. "Compared to the past three years, I'd say you are right, Joseph."

"I'm being serious now. Please come and sit down. I can't talk to your back."

Anne stopped washing the dishes and dried her hands as she turned to face him. The look on his face frightened her. "What is it? What's wrong?"

He managed a half smile with some effort. "Nothing's wrong. I just want to talk to you."

"All right. I'm listening."

She waited, but he didn't say anything. He had his hands deep in his pockets as he shifted his weight from one foot to the other.

She folded her arms, giving him her complete attention.

He glanced at her face and suddenly crossed to the stove. "A cup of *coffe* would be *goot* right now. Would you like one?" He pulled a mug from her cabinet and began filling it from her coffeepot.

"*Nay*, I'm fine. Help yourself. What is it that you wanted to talk to me about?" Something was very odd. She had never seen him look so nervous.

"*Koom* and sit at the table." He settled in a chair.

She pulled out the one across from him and sat down. "All right, I'm sitting. Joseph, what is going on?"

He took a sip of his coffee and then gripped the mug between his fingers. His knuckles stood out white. "My farm is small, but I have room for expansion in my milking parlor. I could double my goat herd if I had someone to help me."

"Twice as many goats next door? Ack, I would not be overjoyed. No wonder you wanted me to sit down." She didn't bother to hide her sarcasm.

He cleared his throat. "I'm trying to tell you that I can support a family."

"That's good, since you already have one child."

"You have hit the nail on the head. I already have a child."

"And?"

"You love Leah. I can see that. You are like a mother to her. She will never remember Fannie."

Anne dropped her gaze to stare at her hands. "I do love Leah, with all my heart."

Joseph reached across the table and took Anne's hand in his. Startled, her gaze shot to his face. "You want what is best for her. So do I. I think it is best that she have a *mudder*."

"She has a *mudder*."

"*Nay*, she does not. I received a letter from Fannie this morning. She is never coming home. She wants me to raise Leah. I can't do that by myself. I need a helpmate. Someone who will love Leah as a mother loves a child."

Anne had no idea where this conversation was going. "Are you trying to tell me that you have decided to marry?"

Relief filled his eyes. "*Ja*. That is exactly what I'm trying to say."

Anne blinked hard as his words settled in her mind. He was going to take a wife. That would change everything. He wouldn't need a nanny. He wouldn't need her.

When he married, she would have no part in Leah's life except as the kindly woman next door. Of course, she expected Leah to grow up. In a few years, she would have no need for a *kindt heedah*. She would start school and soon be old enough to take care of herself.

Tears stung the back of Anne's eyes. She'd thought she would be able to hold her darling girl and sing her to sleep until that time. She'd thought she had years to enjoy her baby, to watch her grow up. Now Joseph was telling her another woman would take her place.

How would she bear being alone again without her baby to brighten each day?

She fumbled for the right words to say. "I wish you every happiness, Joseph. Who have you chosen?"

"I've chosen you."

Anne snatched her hand away from him. Was he out of his mind? "What do you mean by that?"

"I knew I wouldn't do this right. I'm sorry. Anne, will you do me the honor of becoming my wife? Will you become Leah's *mudder*? My farm is small, and so is yours. If we combine them, we will have more than enough for one family."

"You want me to marry you so that you can have my farm?" She drew back to glare at him. She didn't know if she was outraged or simply floored by his audacity.

"Not for the farm, but you must admit it makes sense. You are a reasonable woman."

"I thought I was until this minute."

It seemed to dawn on him that he had made a mistake. "Please, Anne. Hear me out. I like you a great deal. I hope I have not offended you. I think that you like me, too. We have become friends. *Goot* friends. Many a marriage has started with less and prospered. We both love Leah. Together we can give her all that she needs. Will you consider my offer?"

He liked her, but he hadn't said that he loved her. Her feelings for him had grown by leaps and bounds in the past few weeks. It hurt that he didn't return them. "Friendship isn't enough to hold a marriage together."

"Isn't it? It's what binds a man and woman together. Love is like a bonfire. It burns bright and hot, but it dies down. The glowing embers of the fire are what give the warmth that lets a person draw near and use the fire. To heat a home. To cook a meal. To forge iron. Friendship is like those embers. It sustains us."

Anne rose to her feet and crossed the kitchen to the sink. She gripped the edge and bowed her head. Would it be so wrong to accept him? She loved him, but could she spend a lifetime with a man who didn't love her in return?

She would have Leah, too, as her very own babe to love and care for her entire life.

Joseph might not love her now, but perhaps he could learn to love her over time. If she said no, he would look elsewhere for a wife and she would have to watch another woman become the center of his life. How could she bear that?

He came to stand behind her and placed his hands on her shoulders. He was so close she could feel his warmth. If she leaned back, she would be in his arms. Wasn't that where she wanted to be?

She had been given a choice. She could move into his arms or remain alone for the rest of her life and grow old with no one to care for her or about her.

Leah began fussing in the other room. The

overwhelming urge to go comfort the child made up Anne's mind.

But before she agreed to become Joseph's wife, she needed to tell him about her shameful past. She dreaded the look of condemnation that would fill his eyes, but it wasn't fair to try and keep her secret from him now. Not even if it cost her everything.

She drew a deep breath and turned around. "Before I give you an answer, there are some things you need to know about me."

A half smile tilted his lips. "I know as much about you as I need to know. You are kind. You are hardworking. You are a woman of faith. A little bossy perhaps, but you love Leah."

"You must listen to me. There was a time when I was not such a good woman. I was a foolish teenage girl who fell in love with the wrong man."

His grin disappeared. "Was this during your *rumspringa*? Before you were baptized?"

"Ja." She closed her eyes as shame burned in her chest.

"Have you violated the Ordnung, the rules of our church, since you took your vows?" he asked softly.

She opened her eyes so he could read the truth in them. "*Nay*, I have not."

He laid a finger to her lips as his gaze softened. "Then there is no need to speak of the past."

"You have a right to know."

"That is between you and God. The sins of your past were forgiven. I have made mistakes, too. I have done things that displeased the Lord, but I sought forgiveness and it was given to me. Our souls were made new through baptism."

Anne's heart swelled with love. She could not ask for a better mate in life. Joseph was a good man in every sense of the word. She would be blessed to be his wife. Was this God's plan for them? How could she know? How could she be sure she was doing the right thing?

She prayed for an answer and felt it deep in her soul. She placed a hand on his chest and felt the heavy thud of his heart against her palm.

"I will wed you, Joseph Lapp. I'll strive to be a good wife to you and a good mother to Leah."

He covered her hand with his own. "Leah needs us both. This is the best thing for her."

Anne nodded and bit her lip as trepidation filled her heart. Was a marriage without love between the parents really the best thing for a child?

Chapter Nineteen

Their intention to marry was published in church the Sunday after Joseph proposed. Simeon Shetler and Dinah Plank's intentions were published the same day and caused more of a stir than Anne and Joseph's announcement. Anne's wedding would take place a week before Thanksgiving. Dinah and Simeon would marry the first Tuesday in December.

Anne expected her friends to be surprised by her engagement, but most of them weren't. Ellen Beachy Shetler expressed it best. "The gossip about you and Joseph has been circulating for weeks. We all knew something was up. We're all happy for you."

A whirlwind of activity began for Anne the next day. Invitations were sent to her far-flung relatives. She didn't have a big family, only a few cousins in Ohio. She didn't expect many of them to come, but she hoped they would. She sent another set of invitations to her friends and Joseph's friends in Honeysuckle. She also sent them to a few of the nurses at the hospital in Lancaster, including Roxann. They had been instrumental in helping her improve her midwifery skills and in caring for Rhonda Yoder and her son.

Naomi Beiler offered the use of her home for the wedding ceremony and Anne gratefully accepted since her mother was gone. The horse Pocahontas was returned to Calvin Miller, and Daisy returned to pulling the buggy, if slowly.

Anne's days were soon filled with sewing her wedding dress, cleaning, cooking and preparations for the big day. She chose a deep blue material for her gown and hoped that Joseph would approve. She saw little of him. He brought Leah over as usual when he was doing his chores, but he didn't stay long. They rarely found time to be alone. It seemed that she always had company.

The day before the wedding, a dozen of her married friends and members of her church arrived to prepare the wedding feast and the house for the bridal party. There would be a generous meal served following the wedding, but the celebration would continue until supper time, when a second meal would be needed for all the guests.

When the day finally arrived, Anne was up at four thirty in the morning. Six of her cousins from Ohio had arrived the night before and were helping her get ready. It was wonderful to see the women she had grown up with and to share stories about old times. It had been a long time since Anne felt so connected to her family.

She was standing at the window looking toward Joseph's house and wondering what he was feeling when Ellen and Lizzie came in to hurry her along. Both of them were newlyweds and the light of happiness in their eyes gave Anne courage. She was doing the right thing, wasn't she? If she married Joseph, he would never have the chance to find a woman he loved. What if he was settling for Anne and regretted it later?

Ellen took Anne's hand. "It's time. Micah has the buggy here for you."

Anne had asked Ellen and Neziah to be members of her bridal party. Micah, Neziah's brother, was acting as *hostler*, the driver for the group.

Anne nodded. She was ready, but her fingers were as cold as ice. Was Leah reason enough to wed Joseph and be bound to him for all time?

Ellen squeezed Anne's hand. "It will be fine."

Anne took a deep breath and her panic retreated. Leah was only part of the reason for this day. She might have been instrumental in bringing them together, but it was Anne's love that would make them a family. With God's help, she would be a good wife and mother.

Joseph was waiting for her at the foot of the stairs. He looked every bit as nervous as she felt, but he also looked incredibly handsome in his new black suit and bow tie. Her husband-to-be had Leah in his arms. He smiled and held out his hand. "Are you ready?"

She grasped his fingers tightly. "I am. Are you?"

"Maybe."

"Now is the time to run," she suggested.

"*Nay*, you are stuck with me."

"*Goot*. Are Rhonda and Silas here?" She and Joseph had asked them to be their second bridal-party couple.

"They are outside in the buggy already," Neziah answered. He slapped Joseph on the back. "Better get going."

The trip to Naomi's home didn't take long. The wedding-party couples rode in a second buggy while the bride and groom rode alone. Anne sat stiffly beside Joseph. She was grateful to have Leah on her lap because she wasn't sure if she should hold his hand or not. Her wedding day was something she would remember all her life. She didn't want it marred by these doubts.

As if he could read her thoughts, he leaned toward her and whispered in her ear. "Smile. You look like you're going to a funeral."

"I'm sorry. I'm not sure how to act."

He took her hand between his own. "Act like yourself."

"You mean throw a tomato at you?"

He threw back his head and laughed. "That was a *goot* throw. You sure did surprise me that day."

Micah glanced over his shoulder at them but didn't comment.

Anne lowered her voice. "I was so mad at you. I hope you have forgiven me."

"I have. And I hope you have forgiven me

for causing you so much extra work and worry. It was my responsibility to keep my goats out of your garden and I failed. I will not fail you again, Anne. I promise this."

She gazed into his eyes. "We're going to be all right, aren't we?"

"I think so. I really think we are."

She believed him.

It was just after seven o'clock when they arrived at Naomi's home. The pocket doors between her rooms had been pushed open to make room for all the guests, and the benches were being set up.

Abigail came to take charge of Leah while Anne and Joseph greeted the early guests as they arrived. The ceremony wouldn't take place until nine. By eight thirty the wedding party took their places on the benches at the front of the room where the ceremony would be held, Anne with Rhonda and Ellen on one side of the room, Joseph with Silas and Neziah on the other.

Their *forgeher*, or ushers, four married couples from their church group, made sure each guest had a place on one of the long wooden benches. When the bishop entered the room, he motioned for Anne and Joseph to come with him as the congregation began singing.

Anne and Joseph glanced at each other and quietly followed the bishop. It was customary for the bishop or ministers to counsel the couple before the ceremony took place. One of Naomi's bedrooms had been prepared with chairs for them all. Anne's knees were shaking.

Holding open the door, Bishop Andy said, "Sit. Be of good heart, for I promise not to keep you long."

He took a seat in front of them. "Anne, your place will now be at your husband's side. You will be his counselor, his helpmate. God willing, you will bear his children and raise them to love and serve the Lord."

"That is my hope," she said softly. The thought of having more children filled her with joy, but being a true wife to Joseph filled her with concern. Her hands grew cold.

The bishop cleared his throat. "Joseph, you must provide for and cherish your wife. Anne's love and God's love will be your strength in times of trial. As happy as you are today, it is hard to imagine the sorrows you will face together and alone. We are but travelers through this world on our way to eternal joy at the foot of God's throne. No matter how great is the sorrow or joy that this life brings, it will pass away and the glory of God will shine all around you. Do you understand this?"

Joseph nodded. "I do and I accept what God wills."

The bishop smiled at him and turned to Anne. "*Gottes* love is never wavering, never changing and never ending. Remember this in times of trouble."

"I will," she said quietly.

"Marriage is not easy, but it can be wonderful. I pray God will bless you both. Shall we go back in?"

Anne reached for Joseph's hand. He gave her fingers a quick squeeze. Soon they would be joined as husband and wife. She wanted the man with stormy eyes to be hers alone and it was about to happen. Her heart soared with excitement and happiness as they followed the bishop into the main room and returned to their places.

The singing continued, punctuated by sermons from the ministers, for almost three hours. Anne tried to keep her mind on what was being said, but she could only think about the coming days and nights when she would become a true wife to Joseph.

Finally, Bishop Andy stood to address the congregation. "Brothers and sisters, we are gathered here in Christ's name for a solemn purpose. Joseph Lapp and Anne Stoltzfus are about to make irrevocable vows. This is a most serious step and not to be taken lightly, for it is a lifelong commitment to love and cherish one another."

As the bishop continued at length, Anne glanced at Joseph. He was sitting up straight, listening to every word. He didn't look the least bit nervous. The bishop motioned for Anne and Joseph to come forward.

As Anne stood before him with Joseph at her side, she knew the questions that would be asked of her.

Looking at them both, the bishop said, "Do you confess and believe God has ordained marriage to be a union between one man and one woman? And do you believe that you are approaching this marriage in accordance with His wishes and in the way you have been taught?"

She and Joseph both answered, "Yes."

Turning to Joseph, the bishop asked, "Do

you believe, brother, that God has provided this woman as a marriage partner for you?"

"I do believe it." Joseph smiled at her and her heart beat faster.

The bishop then turned to her. "Do you believe, sister, that God has provided this man as a marriage partner for you?"

"I do."

"Joseph, do you also promise Anne that you will care for her in sickness or bodily weakness as befits a Christian husband? Do you promise you will love, forgive and be patient with her until God separates you by death?"

"I do so promise," Joseph answered solemnly.

The bishop asked Anne the same questions. She focused on Joseph. He was waiting for her answer, too. Taking a deep breath, she nodded. "I promise."

The bishop took her hand, placed it in Joseph's hand and covered their fingers with his own. "The God of Abraham, of Isaac and of Jacob be with you. May He bestow His blessings richly upon you through Jesus Christ, amen."

That was it. They were man and wife.

A final prayer ended the ceremony and

the festivities began. The couple returned to Anne's home, where the women of the congregation began preparing the wedding meal in the kitchen. The men had arranged tables in a U shape around the walls of the living room.

In the corner of the room facing the front door, the honored place, the *eck*, meaning the corner table, was quickly set up for the wedding party.

He was married. It was hard to wrap his mind around the fact. When the table was ready, Joseph took his place with his groomsmen seated to his right. Anne was ushered in and took her seat at his left-hand side. It symbolized the place she would occupy in his buggy and in his life. A helpmate, always at his side. Her cheeks were rosy red and her eyes sparkled with happiness. There would be a long day of celebration and feasting, but tonight would come, and she would be his alone. Could he make her happy? Under the table, he squeezed her hand. She gave him a shy smile in return.

Joseph released Anne's hand and began to speak to the people who filed past. The single men were arranged along the table to his right and the single women were arranged along the tables to Anne's left. Later, at the evening meal, the unmarried people would be paired up according to the bride and groom's choosing, as Amish weddings were where matchmaking often got started.

Although most Amish wedding feasts went on until long after dark, Joseph still had a dairy to run and goats to milk. He and Anne bid their guests good night before dark and walked toward his home. He carried Leah, who was worn out and sleeping after such a long day.

His heart filled with trepidation as he glanced at the woman beside him. She was not just his neighbor. She was now Mrs. Joseph Lapp. His wife. His helpmate, until death did part them. His soul mate for eternity. Had he done the right thing in convincing her to marry him?

He believed so. Together they would build a good life together. She would be a loving mother to Leah. He would do his best to be a good husband to her and show her just how much he cared for her. The thought made him smile.

Anne gripped his hand. "What are you smiling about?"

"What are *you* smiling about?" he countered.

Her smile trembled. "I asked you first."

"I was thinking about adding another milking parlor in the barn." He glanced to see if she was buying his story.

"Why would we need another milking parlor?" She looked at him askew.

"So you can have your own herd to milk."

"Me? I've no wish to have my own herd. Yours is trouble enough."

"After all this time, you still don't like my goats? Maybe we should have discussed this before the wedding." He wanted to see her smiling a bright smile, not this scared, timid one.

"The young ones are cute. The does are sweet natured, but I will never be fond of those smelly bucks."

"Not even Chester?"

"Especially not Chester. If you wish to give me a bridal gift, you can give Chester away."

He laughed out loud. She wasn't going to be a boring wife, that was for certain. He saw her relax.

A growing nervousness suddenly replaced his humor. Would he be a good husband? Could he make her happy? Could he give her children? Could he grow old beside her and still care for her?

He prayed that he could do all within his power to make her happy. She had married him for Leah's sake, but he prayed she would grow to love him in time. Even just a little.

As they walked through the gate, he saw a car parked in front of the house. He didn't recognize it. "Anne, do you know them? Are they some of your *Englisch* friends?"

"I don't think so, but it could be someone from the hospital in Lancaster. I sent several of the obstetrical nurses there an invitation."

"There's no one in the car. They must be making themselves at home."

He smiled at her. "Did I tell you what a pretty bride you made?"

She blushed a charming shade of pink and took the baby from him. "*Nay*, you didn't mention it."

"I reckon I had a lot on my mind."

She gave him a saucy grin. "Like how to bolt before the knot was tied?"

"I can honestly say that never crossed my mind."

At the sound of the door opening, Joseph glanced toward the house. Fannie came running out. "Leah! Oh, my beautiful baby! I thought I would never see you again." She pulled the child from Anne's arms.

Chapter Twenty

Anne stood frozen with shock. This was her nightmare come to life. She held the baby in her arms, ready to love her for a lifetime, and then the child was torn away from her.

Was this Fannie? Leah's mother? She looked to Joseph for confirmation.

He looked as stunned as she was. "Fannie, what are you doing here?"

So it was his sister. Anne saw her dreams of a lifetime with Leah and Joseph crumble to dust.

Fannie looked at her brother with a trembling smile. "I couldn't do it. I couldn't stay away from her. I tried. I tried so hard. But it's okay. I can take care of her now." She gestured to a young man standing behind her. "This is

Brian. He wants us to be a family. He knows I need my baby to make me happy."

Anne wrapped her arms tightly across her middle to ease the crippling ache. She wanted to snatch Leah back. She wanted to take her and run far away. What right did Fannie have to show up and expect Joseph to give the child back to her?

"Don't do this, Fannie." His voice wavered. His hands were shaking. Anne took hold of one. She needed something solid to hold on to or she would scream.

Fannie tipped her head to the side. "Don't do what, Joe?"

"Don't take her away from us."

Taking a step back, Fannie held Leah tightly. The baby started to cry. "She's my daughter. I need her. I wanted you to look after her for a little while. That's what I told you."

"Your letter said you weren't coming back. I didn't want to believe it, but then you sent another letter telling me I would never hear from you again. She is ours now, Fannie. This is my wife, Anne. We love Leah. Please don't do this to us. Don't take her away."

"I'm sorry. I was mixed up. I didn't know what to do."

The man she called Brian stepped up and put an arm around her shoulders. "Johnny was a real piece of work. He broke her wrist. He even shook the baby. Fannie gave her baby to you to protect her. Now she's safe. They are both safe with me. I'm gonna take care of them."

Fannie looked at him. "Johnny didn't mean to hurt me. It was just that Leah cried all the time. She wouldn't stop."

"She was allergic to her formula," Anne said. "That's why she cried so much. She has to have goat's milk now."

Brian sneered. "Goat's milk? Who ever heard of that? We'll take her to a pediatrician. There are all kinds of formulas out there. There has to be something better than goat's milk."

"There's nothing wrong with it, Brian. I grew up drinking it." Fannie tried to comfort Leah, but the baby only cried louder.

"You didn't know any better because you belonged to a backward religious group who thinks we should all live in the Dark Ages."

"No, we don't," Anne countered.

"Whatever. We should get going, Fannie. Can't you make her stop crying?"

Anne pressed her hands to her heart. It was over. She was losing another beloved child.

Why was God doing this to her? She could feel her heart withering inside her. Why wasn't Joseph doing something to stop it? She glanced at his face. His gray eyes were blank. His face looked as if it had been turned to stone except for the tracks of his tears. She had never seen such pain.

Leah continued to cry. Anne needed to help her. "She's just hungry. I will get a bottle for her. Come inside, everyone. Fannie, you can feed her while I pack her things."

"We don't need your cheap homemade stuff," Brian said. "I can buy her whatever she needs in a real store."

Fannie turned pleading eyes to him. "Let me feed her, and then we'll go. She'll sleep in the car the whole way if she gets something to eat first."

"All right, but don't let these hicks talk you into leaving her. You're easily persuaded to make the wrong choices. That's why I'm here for you. To be your backbone."

"I won't let them change my mind."

Anne forgave Brian for his insults but she wanted to shake Fannie. What was she doing with such a man? Why was she letting him insult her family? Anne turned to Joseph. "Come inside. Visit with your sister for a while."

"I don't have a sister. She is dead to me."

"*Brooder,* do not say that. Please!" Fannie reached for him.

Joseph jerked away from her and walked out to the barn.

"Speak English, honey. This is America. Is that the shunning thing the Amish do?" Brian asked.

Fannie's eyes filled with tears. "He didn't mean that. I know he didn't mean that."

Anne took her by the elbow and led her inside Joseph's house. Brian paused in the doorway. "I'll wait in the car."

Fannie sat down at the kitchen table. "Did I hear Joseph right? Did he say you are his wife?"

"*Ja.*" Anne forced herself to go through the motions of warming a bottle for Leah one last time. She began filling up a pan with hot water.

"That's good. He needs somebody. It has to be lonely out here all by himself."

She took a bottle from the refrigerator and placed it in the pan. "Your brother was lonely. He missed you very much. He has his ani-

mals—you know how much he likes them—
but he loves you."

She turned to face Fannie. Leah was arching
away from her mother and reaching for Anne.
Anne bit her lip so hard she tasted blood. How
could this be happening?

"Joseph did his duty by raising me, but he
never really loved me."

"How can you say that?"

"He was always gone. He left me alone all
the time. It was my fault Beth was killed. I
made her trade places with me so I could sit
beside him. I loved my brother. I was jealous
of her."

"Joseph didn't blame you, Fannie. He was
gone so much because he was trying to save
this farm. The driver who hit you threatened to
sue and take the farm if Joseph didn't pay for
the damages to his vehicle. Joseph believed the
accident was his fault."

"I didn't know that. Why didn't he tell me?"

"You were a child. He didn't want to worry
you." Anne checked the bottle's temperature
by shaking a few drops on her wrist. It was
warm enough. She handed the bottle to Fannie,
although she longed to hold Leah once more.

"*Danki.* I mean, thanks. Brian doesn't like it when I speak *Deitsch.*"

"Are you sure he is the man for you? He doesn't speak kindly to you. It makes me worry. We are sisters now. We must look out for each other."

"Brian doesn't hit me. But I'm not very bright. I'm not educated. That frustrates him."

Anne couldn't believe she was sending Leah into such a poor situation. How could she bear knowing her beautiful child would be raised by that unkind man?

Fannie gave Leah her bottle. After fighting it briefly, the baby latched on and drank eagerly. "Wow, she really likes the goat's milk. She would never eat like this for me. I felt like such a failure as a mother."

Anne sat beside her and laid a hand on her arm. "It wasn't anything you did, Fannie. Eventually, your doctor would have figured out what was wrong."

"Johnny never let me take her to the doctor. He said they were a waste of time and money."

"Johnny doesn't sound like a very smart man."

Fannie chuckled. "He wasn't and he wasn't a good musician, either."

"Where are you staying? I would love to keep in touch. Find out how Leah is doing, you know. We wanted to send you an invitation to the wedding, but your letters didn't have a return address."

"I would have liked to come. I'm not sure Brian will let me write to you. Besides, Joseph says I'm dead to him. He won't read my letters, even if I write."

"I'll read them. You haven't been shunned by the church. You aren't under the Ban. Can you at least tell me which city you live in?"

"Lancaster."

"That's not too far away. I have a friend there. Let me give you her name." Anne found a piece of paper. Quickly, she wrote Roxann's name and phone number. "Roxann Shield works at Lancaster Medical Center. She's a midwife like I am, only she's a nurse-midwife. If you ever need medical advice or if Leah gets sick, Roxann will see you free of charge."

Anne knew Roxann wouldn't be able to do that, but she would forward the bill to Anne.

"That's nice. Thanks. Leah, you little piglet, you're almost done with this bottle."

Tears pricked the back of Anne's eyes. *Slow*

down, baby. When you're done, I may never see you again.

She cleared her throat and began gathering items to put in Leah's bag. "I'm going to put a few things in here for her. Diapers and such. I know you'll buy new clothes, but this will get you home. I'll put in the recipe for her formula, too. You can buy goat's milk in most stores. In case you can't find another formula that works."

Brian appeared in the doorway. "I'm getting tired of waiting. How long does it take two Amish women to feed a baby?"

"She's done." Fannie jumped to her feet.

Anne closed her eyes. This couldn't happen. "Please don't take her. We'll give her the best possible home. We love her."

"I love her, too. I've got to go." Fannie started out the door.

Anne switched to *Deitsch*. "Little sister, you will always have a home with us, even if you remain *Englisch*. You are loved by us and by God. Never forget that. Do not fear to come to us."

Brian frowned. "What is she jabbering about?"

"She's just wishing me a safe journey. It's a tradition. Let's go."

Anne's heart broke into a million pieces. She followed them to the door, praying for Fannie to change her mind. Praying for God to intervene and stop her. But they got in the car and drove away.

She wanted to scream and cry, but a strange calm settled over her. It was as if some part of her mind disconnected from her emotions. She became dead inside. The pain was too deep for tears.

She turned back into the house, then went to the bedroom she would share with Joseph and took off her wedding dress. Carefully, she folded it away. She would wear it again only when her body was dressed for her burial. She put on one of her everyday dresses that had been brought over by her attendants and then she sat down on the sofa in Joseph's living room and waited for him to come in.

At midnight she gave up trying to stay awake and went to bed. When she woke just before dawn, she was still alone.

Joseph raised his head and rubbed his stiff neck. He'd slept slumped over his desk in his office. He hadn't actually slept. The night had been more a series of fitful rest, terrifying dreams and an even more terrible reality. He had tried to pray, but he found no comfort in speaking to God. God wasn't listening.

He rose stiffly and walked to the front of the barn. Smoke rose from the chimney of the house. Anne must be up. He leaned against the doorway and closed his eyes. It didn't stop him from seeing the mess he'd made of their lives.

He should have gone to her last night. He should have tried to comfort her, but he didn't know how. She had married him for Leah's sake and now Leah was gone. His grand idea to build a family had turned into a trap for Anne. She didn't have the baby she loved and she was stuck with a husband she didn't love, either. The irony was a bitter pill to swallow first thing in the morning. He hadn't gone to Anne last night because he was a coward. He was afraid she would turn him away. And he didn't know if he could survive that.

"I was beginning to worry about you."

He jerked upright. She was standing a few feet away looking sad and yet still beautiful in the early-morning light. She wore a dark blue dress with a black apron. Somber colors for a somber day. "I'm sorry, Anne."

"I know. This isn't what we bargained for, is it?"

"*Nay*. It isn't. I'm going to milk. You can go home if you want. We'll think of what to tell people later."

"I am home, Joseph."

"I meant you could go to your own house if you wished."

She folded her arms tightly across her middle. Her chin quivered as her head came up. "I know full well what you meant. We are wed. A promise is a promise, but promises can be broken. Our vows cannot be unspoken. They were made before God and man. I'm your wife."

"Leah was the reason for those vows. Now she's gone. I knew better than to love that child." He couldn't bear to be reminded of what he'd lost. The child he loved, the sister he would have given anything to help, his dreams of a family, of a wife who could learn to love him. They were all ashes in his mouth. He turned away and began walking toward the barn.

"I miss her, too. My heart is breaking, the

way yours is breaking, because I love her, too," Anne yelled. "All we have left is each other."

He spun around. "Would you have married me if you knew Fannie was coming back for Leah?"

She pressed her lips tightly together, unable to answer him. She didn't have to. He already knew the answer. "Go home or stay. It makes no difference to me."

"We have to start somewhere, Joseph."

"I know. I'm just not ready to do that yet." He walked away without looking back.

He was in so much pain. Anne knew he was suffering and she was powerless to help. She understood the pain of losing a child. Not once but twice. Time and faith in God's mercy were the only things that would heal Joseph's wounds. And hers.

She returned to the house and walked into the living room. Leah's crib with its bright quilt sat where it had been yesterday. Yesterday it held a happy, grinning baby girl. Today it held only memories.

Anne ran her hands along the smooth wooden rail. Great care had gone into creating it. The owner would want it back. There would be children and grandchildren to use it and that was a good thing. Love should be passed down in families, too.

She opened the drawers of the dresser and took out the outfits that Leah had worn. She held them to her face, but they had been washed. They didn't hold her baby's scent. They smelled of fresh air and sunshine, just as they had when she took them off the clothesline. She sat down on the floor and gathered them into a pile on her lap. The tears came then and there was no stopping them.

She didn't know how long she sat there crying, but she felt Joseph sink down beside her. He gathered her into his arms and held her as she wept. His tears mingled with hers. They were two souls broken by grief. Where did they go from there?

Chapter Twenty-One

When their tears were spent, Joseph rose to his feet, wiped his face with his hands and went to the crib. "Do you want me to put these things away?"

"I can do it for you. I know how hard it is to put away a child's things. I remember packing away the quilt I made for him was the hardest thing for me."

"Whose quilt?" He asked without looking at her.

"My son's."

"Your son?" Joseph was clearly bewildered. "You had a child?"

"I tried to tell you the day you proposed, but you said it didn't matter. I was grateful that I didn't have to share my shameful story with you, but I want you to hear the story now."

"All right."

"I was seventeen and in love with the son of the banker in the town near where I lived in Ohio. I was incredibly foolish and naive. I make no excuse for myself. I knew what we were doing was wrong, but I loved him so much. When I told him I was pregnant, everything changed. I thought we would marry. I was badly mistaken. He didn't want to be a husband or a father. He had plans to go away to college, and he wasn't going to give that up for a silly Amish girl. He wanted me to place our baby for adoption."

"He was a man without honor."

"He was a frightened boy pressured by his parents. I forgave him long ago. My mother was the midwife in our community. She understood, but my father did not. I had shamed him. He wanted nothing to do with me or my child. I was sent to live with my mother's sister. She knew of a childless Amish couple who would love my baby and raise him as their own. It was a heart-wrenching decision, but I finally agreed. That's why I know how hard it must have been for Fannie to leave Leah with you. My heart ached for her. I also know how joyful it was for her to see and hold her baby again."

"I don't wish to talk about my sister. So you gave your child up for adoption?" The timbre of his voice didn't change. Did he disapprove of her actions as he did his sister's?

"I never got the chance. There were complications. My mother did not call the ambulance. My son was born dead because the cord was wrapped around his neck."

"Like Rhonda's babe." His tone softened.

"Very much like that, only *Gott* called my son home. He showed mercy to Rhonda and Silas by sparing their child. I wish I knew why my little Mathias couldn't stay with me. *Gott* has His own plan and we cannot comprehend His ways, but He will have to explain that to me when I stand before Him."

"I'm sorry for all you endured. Now to lose Leah, too. It's not fair."

"We can endure with *Gottes* help. That is why you can't lose faith. *Gott* brought the two of us together because of Leah. His plan has not changed, even though ours have. I will be a good wife to you. I will fulfill my wifely duties. I will honor and obey you all the days of my life, but... I think we both need time to heal."

She folded her hands together and stared at

the floor. "There is a spare bedroom here. I will use that unless you insist otherwise."

Amazed by how calmly Anne spoke about the suffering she had endured, Joseph could only stare at her. Her faith was unwavering. He couldn't say the same. In spite of everything, she had found the strength to go on, to move ahead and to help others by bringing their babies into the world when she had been denied a child of her own. She was a remarkable woman.

He didn't know what to say to her but he knew what he wanted. He wanted a true wife, not a wife in name only.

He wanted Anne. But on her terms.

He wanted her to come to him with love in her heart, not because it was her duty. However long that took, he would wait. Because deep in his soul, he knew she was a woman worth waiting for. The one chosen by God to be his helpmate for life. The woman he had grown to love.

He cleared his throat. "The spare room will be fine. It's never used."

She drew a deep breath. *"Danki."*

He moved to stand in front of her. Placing

his fingers under her chin, he raised her face until she was looking at him. "We were friends before the wedding, Anne. Leah brought us together, but we became friends because of who we are. Not because of her. I want us to be friends now."

A half smile turned up the corner of her lip. "Does that mean you won't make me milk your goats?"

"No, you still have to do that, wife."

Her smile widened. "You make it hard to be your friend."

"If it was easy, everyone would do it."

"I reckon we'll need to be friends if we are to have any kind of marriage at all."

He was glad she could see it that way. For now. "We'll make the best of it. Shall I help you put away these things?"

She touched his arm. "Only if you want to do it."

"I didn't get to say goodbye to her. Maybe this will help."

"We'll pray for her. For both of them."

"I'll pray for Leah, but I'm not sure I can pray for her mother."

"You will. Time heals our wounds even if the scars remain. Leah may yet come back to us, if only for a visit. We can't know what the future holds. Cutting ties with Fannie will cut our ties with Leah, too."

"I know you are right, but I can't condone my sister's choices. It is not an easy thing to shun a person I love, but I do it out of that love. She must see the consequences of her actions and the harm she has caused."

He began picking up the clothes scattered on the floor. Together they packed them away in boxes and stacked them in the crib to be returned to their owners. Later that afternoon he drove the wagon up to the door and loaded Leah's things into it. Anne came out to watch him. He offered his hand. "Would you like to come to town with me?"

She shook her head. "I have enough to do here. I still have things I need to bring over from my place."

"All right. I'll be home for supper. What are we having?"

Crossing her arms, she pretended to look annoyed. "What do you care? You like everything, including pickled okra. You'll like what I put in front of you and you won't complain."

"Spoken like a good wife." He smiled, although he didn't feel like it. He appreciated her efforts to cheer him up. He had tried to do the same for her. It was harder than it looked. They both missed Leah terribly. There was a hole in the fabric of their relationship. He prayed it could be mended.

Driving into town, he had time to contemplate his spunky wife and wonder if she would ever come to care for him. She was used to her independence. He didn't want her to give it up. The last thing he wanted was for their marriage to be a burden to her. He wanted it to be a joy.

He delivered the furniture and other items to Naomi at her home. She was shocked to learn that Leah was no longer with them. He asked her to visit Anne soon. "She is going to need someone to talk to about losing Leah."

"I know she will. I'll be out tomorrow. Bless you both."

The coming night loomed large and awkward when he returned home. They ate a simple supper of bread and cheese and parted company in the center of the living room, where Joseph wished her a good night. He hoped it would be a better night for her. It wouldn't be for him.

Early the next morning, he drove out to see

Calvin Miller. It took a considerable amount of haggling, but he headed for home with Pocahontas tied to the back of his wagon. The pony would be his wedding present to Anne. He knew how much she liked the lively, well-trained little mare and how much she needed a fast buggy horse to get her to her deliveries in time.

She was leaving the henhouse with a basket of eggs in her hand when he drove into the yard. Her eyes lit up with delight when she saw Pocahontas. "Has Calvin decided he can spare her for a few more weeks? That's *wunderbar*."

"You don't have to return her. She's yours now." He stepped down from the wagon.

"You mean you purchased her for me?" Anne's puzzled expression made him chuckle.

He walked around to the rear of the wagon and untied the mare. He led her up to Anne. Taking the egg basket from her, he placed the lead rope in her palm. "She is my wedding gift to you. I don't want my wife being late for a birthing, and Daisy deserves to retire in peace."

Tears glistened in Anne's eyes. "I don't know what to say. This is very kind of you."

Her practical side quickly asserted itself.

"How much did old man Miller charge you for her?"

"You don't want to know."

She opened her mouth to argue, but he forestalled her by holding up his hand. "This bargain is done. I promise that from now on, I will consult you on any purchases because it is your money, too, and we need to manage it wisely. But Pocahontas is a gift."

Anne stroked the horse's nose. "She is one I will cherish, and doubly so because she came from you."

Maybe now was the time to make plans for the future so it didn't feel as if they were simply waiting for Leah to return when she might not. "Next week will be Thanksgiving. I was wondering if you had any plans."

The light in her eyes faded. "Not this year."

"Do you have something you normally do? Somewhere you go? I know a lot of Amish folks enjoy getting together for the *Englisch* holiday."

"I like to invite the families of the babies I've delivered that year over to celebrate. It was something my mother started doing. It's fun to see how the *kinner* have grown."

"Why aren't you doing it this year?"

"Because."

"That's not a reason."

"Because I know you don't like company and crowds. Besides, I don't feel like celebrating now."

It touched him that she was willing to put aside something she enjoyed for his sake. He could surely do the same. "You should invite them, anyway. I would enjoy having a few families at my place for a day."

"Are you sure?"

He knew she loved visiting. Her friends were important to her. She liked people. She especially liked their babies. Maybe having some around in her home would get her to thinking about having children of her own. With him. "I can always go hide in the barn if it gets too rowdy. My office has a lock on the door."

"It does? Why?"

"Beats me. The door came with a lock installed."

"Have you ever used it?"

"Only to prevent Chester from eating my record books."

She grinned, but it quickly faded. "Are you sure you want to do this? People won't be expecting newlyweds to entertain them."

"We've been the unexpected couple from the start. I don't think we should change now. Most newlyweds travel to visit relatives in the months after they wed. You don't have much family. I don't have any..."

He stumbled to a halt. Her eyes filled with sympathy. He drew a deep breath. "Besides, who will milk the goats if I'm not here? I think a Thanksgiving Day feast is exactly what we need to celebrate our marriage."

He smiled, hoping he had convinced her he would enjoy it. He wouldn't, but for her sake, he would pretend to have a wonderful time. Anne deserved things that would make her happy. If it was within his power, he could give her those things. He wanted her to think kindly of him. It occurred to him exactly what he needed to do.

He was going to court his wife.

Anne went through the motions of preparations for Thanksgiving. She welcomed anything to keep her mind off missing Leah, but the baby was never far from her thoughts. She knew the same was true for Joseph, but they were both determined to move forward with their lives. He was as busy as she was, cleaning up the farm, painting his barn. When he wasn't busy with his own projects, he was helping her. As the days passed, their awkwardness eased and their teasing friendship returned.

She hand-delivered two dozen invitations and found many of her families were hoping she would still hold her annual gathering in spite of getting married. All but one family agreed to come, including Rhonda and Silas. Everyone insisted on making it a potluck meal so that Anne and Joseph wouldn't be saddled with the expense of another big dinner so soon after their wedding feast.

Anne scrubbed his house from top to bottom, washing windows and floors. She beat rugs and polished every inch of the furniture. The only room she didn't clean was his bedroom.

Although she was the one who had suggested separate bedrooms, she had secretly hoped he would dismiss her request. It had hurt when he'd agreed. He'd made it clear that he didn't want her, that he didn't love her. Leah had been the only reason he'd proposed. He wanted a mother for his child. Not a wife. She'd known that going in.

Anne was grateful for his friendship, but she wondered how long she could hide the fact that she was deeply in love with him. She longed to tell him the truth, but the fear that he didn't want her love kept her silent. For now, she could hope that his feelings would grow from friendship into something more. If she confessed her love and found he wanted only her friendship, she might die of shame. How pathetic was it to fall in love with another man who didn't want her?

Sometimes, when she caught Joseph staring at her, she thought she saw a deeper affection in the depths of his gray eyes, but he never spoke of it. Maybe she only imagined it.

The evening before Thanksgiving, when Joseph was getting ready to start the evening milking, Anne slipped into her coat and walked out with him.

He gave her a quizzical look. "Where are you going?"

"To help you milk."

"I was there the last time you tried. It wasn't a pretty sight."

"Ha! All I need is a little practice."

"Are you sure you want to try it again?"

"I'm sure."

"Okay, come on." He held out his hand and she took it. It was only a small step forward in their relationship, but she cherished it nonetheless.

Chapter Twenty-Two

The buggies began arriving at ten o'clock in the morning on Thanksgiving. By noon Joseph's house was overflowing with laughing, chattering couples and their babies. Ten families in all had accepted Anne's invitation. The kitchen was awash in mouthwatering aromas. *Hingleflesh*, the roasting chicken, *grumbatta mush*, or mashed potatoes and gravy. There was creamed celery, fried sweet potatoes, macaroni and cheese, and peas. On the counter were pumpkin and lemon sponge pies and trays of cookies. Occasionally, one or two of the older children attempted to sample some, but they were quickly herded out of the kitchen.

Joseph found himself surrounded by young men who were happy to tease him about his recent nuptials. He smiled at their jokes and tolerated their ribbing, never letting on that he and Anne still had separate bedrooms.

Anne was in her element. Several times during the day, he caught her eye and she gave him a bright smile, the first one in days. These women were her friends and she enjoyed being the hostess. At one point in the late afternoon, he noticed she was missing from the group. Some of the families were getting ready to leave and he knew she would want to say goodbye. He cornered Rhonda. "Have you seen Anne?"

"She took the baby into the other room to change him for me."

"Danki," he said, going in search of his missing wife. Joseph opened the door to her bedroom and saw her seated in the rocker, holding Rhonda's infant snuggled against her chest. Her cheek lay on the top of the baby's head. A single tear rolled from the corner of her eye.

She looked up. "I miss her so much. My arms are empty without her."

He came and knelt in front of her. He laid his hand on the baby's head. "I miss her, too. I can't stop thinking about her. Is she okay? Is Fannie taking good care of her? I'm afraid

I will wonder what has become of her for my whole life."

"I'm sorry that you married me in haste and are stuck with me now." Another tear slipped down her face.

His heart ached for her. He moved his hand to cup her cheek. "Oh, Anne, please don't say that. I am *not* sorry that I married you."

"Do you mean that?" Her eyes begged him for the truth.

He struggled to find the words that would convince her. "I mean it with all my heart. Perhaps this was God's plan for Leah all along. She was our matchmaker. I would not have gone looking for a wife otherwise."

Anne nodded. "I would've never considered you husband material if not for her."

A glow of hope centered itself in his chest. "Husband material? Do you think you can mold me into a man who will make you happy?"

"*Nay*, I cannot do that. I would not change a single thing about you. You already make me happy."

He wanted that to be true, but he knew he was no prize. "I am not as handsome as Micah. Nor as witty or charming."

"But you have something he doesn't have."

"One hundred goats?" he asked, trying to coax a smile from her. It worked.

"Even if he acquired two hundred goats, he would still not possess what you already hold."

"And what is that?"

"My heart and my love."

Happiness exploded in his heart and sent a lump into his throat. He didn't deserve her love.

She looked down. "I didn't mean to burden you with this so soon. I know you don't love me and that's okay. I was going to wait until you came to care for me, too, before I spoke."

Her gaze rose to his face. "But then I thought what if I lost you as I lost Leah and I never told you that I loved you. I couldn't stand that."

Anne stroked the baby's head and let the infant curl his fingers around her pinkie. It helped to hold another baby. At first she didn't think it would, but Leah had taught her that she could love more than one child. Joseph had shown her she could love more than one man, even if he didn't love her in return.

Joseph cleared his throat. "Anne, if I possessed nothing else in the world but your heart and your love, I would be the richest man on earth. I love you, too."

Her eyes widened in wonder. "You do?"

He bent toward her and kissed her forehead. "I think I've loved you since the day you hit me with a tomato."

She gave him a wavery smile as joy unfurled in her heart. What had she done to deserve such a wonderful man? "If that is what it takes to get your attention, I'm going to plant a lot of tomatoes in the spring."

He grinned, but then his smile faded and his eyes grew serious.

Joseph knew he had to make a complete confession. This would the start of their true marriage. From now on, there could only be honesty between them. "Darling, I tricked you into marrying me."

"I don't understand."

"The bishop said he would take Leah away if I didn't find a wife. He said he would give her to a childless couple to raise. I couldn't bear to lose her. I knew how much you loved her, and I used that love to convince you to marry me. Can you forgive me for that?"

"There is nothing to forgive. We both loved her."

The bedroom door opened and Rhonda came in. Joseph rose to his feet and curbed his need to show Anne just how much he cared. He would bide his time for now, but when they were alone he would pour out his heart to her.

Rhonda said, "Silas is getting ready to go home. I thought I should collect my baby before we leave."

"I reckon I have to give him back." Anne kissed the top of the baby's head and handed him to her mother. She and Joseph followed the young mother outside, where her husband had their buggy hitched and waiting for her.

A car drove in and stopped beyond the buggy. The driver-side door opened and an *Englisch* woman stepped out.

"Roxann," Anne cried and rushed toward her. The two women embraced. "Joseph, come and meet my friend Roxann Shield. She is the nurse-midwife I have been telling you about."

Roxann nodded to him. "It's a pleasure to meet you."

"Our Thanksgiving meal is over, but there is plenty left to eat. Come in." He tipped his head toward the house, realizing that he had enjoyed the day visiting with people he knew and even those he didn't. There would be more get-togethers in their future. His future. One with Anne by his side and God willing, children of their own around them.

"Actually, I've just come to deliver a package," Roxann said.

"A package?" Anne gave her a puzzled look.

"It's really two packages." She leaned down and spoke to someone in the car. "I brought you this far. The next step is up to you."

The passenger-side door opened and a woman stepped out. Joseph realized it was Fannie. And she held Leah in her arms. She glanced at Joseph and then looked down. *"Hallo, brooder."*

He took a step back, too stunned to speak.

Anne could barely believe her eyes. Leah was here. God had given her the chance to see her beautiful baby again. Anne glanced at Fannie. Why was she here? And why was she with Roxann? Anne turned to Joseph. She could not invite Fannie in without his consent. He had declared that his sister was dead to him and he was the head of the house.

"Why are you here?" he demanded.

Fannie turned to Roxann. "Maybe this was a bad idea."

"No, I think this was the best idea you have

had in a long time. Give him a chance," Roxann said.

Anne looked to her friend. "Roxann, what's going on?"

"Fannie can tell you. Go ahead."

Staring at the ground, Fannie began speaking. "After Johnny dumped me, I was desperate. He took all our money. I stole some stuff and got caught. That's when I wrote the second letter to Joseph. The judge gave me probation instead of jail time. I met Brian there. He was on probation, too. We hit it off, or so I thought."

Roxann looked to Joseph. "Brian was on probation for domestic abuse. He hit his previous girlfriend."

"I didn't like the way he talked to you," Joseph said.

Anne struggled to quell her mounting excitement. At least he was speaking to his sister. "How did you meet Roxann?"

"You gave me her name. I thought I was pregnant again, so I got an appointment with her. You said she would see me for free. I had just left Brian. I was worried he'd hurt Leah. I think I finally wised up about guys like him. I don't know why I always find them."

Roxann smiled at Anne. "By the way, you owe me one hundred and seventy-five dollars for an office visit."

"I'll write you a check." Anne lowered her voice. "Fannie, are you pregnant?"

She nodded. "Johnny is the father. It's dumb, I know, but I just want someone to love me. Someone to hold."

Anne held out her arms. "We love you and your babies."

"You don't even know me."

"I know you," Joseph said. "And I have always loved you. *Willkomm* home, little sister. Promise me you will stay as long as you need."

Tears rolled down Fannie's face. "That might be a really long time." She flew to her brother's arms and Anne gave thanks to God for His kindness.

"Can I have my old room?" Fannie asked when she stopped crying.

"I have a few things of mine in there, but *ja*," Anne answered. "Roxann, please come in and I'll fix you something to eat."

"I don't mind if I do. It was a long ride." Roxann followed Fannie inside.

Joseph put his arm around Anne. "That leaves us with just one problem."

"I know."

"We only have one bedroom left."

"I realize that." Her cheeks grew hot.

"I'm willing to share my space with my wife. Are you ready to come home?"

She threw her arms around his neck. "I've never been so ready in my life. *Gott* has granted us a great gift."

"He has, but there is one more thing I need."

"What?"

"A kiss, Mrs. Lapp. I need to find out if my wife is a good kisser."

Anne glanced toward the house. They were still alone if she didn't count the dozens of goats watching them over the fences. "I have no idea if I'm a good kisser, but I'm willing to practice until I get it right."

"*Goot* girl." He proceeded to pull her close and kiss her tenderly.

Joy flooded every fiber of her being. She put her arms around his neck and drew him closer. "I can see I'm going to need a lot of practice."

"Tonight. But right now I want to go hold my baby girl."

"Me, too." They linked arms and entered the house with joyful hearts.

Epilogue

Early March

"We've got twins!" Anne shouted to Joseph.

"Twins? I'm coming." He jogged across the pasture to her side. A young doe was nursing two brown-and-black kids with white stars on their foreheads and long floppy ears.

"*Goot* girl, Jenny. Two nice little *bubbels*." He patted her head as she nuzzled her newborns.

"Is this the last of them?" Anne wiped her hands on a towel and gazed out over the greening pasture dotted with does and wobbly kids. A hedge of honeysuckle was blooming on an old rock fence nearby and the air was sweet with the scent.

"Jenny was the last one. We have fifty-two new goats. Your own milk herd in another two years."

She smiled at the love of her life. He still liked goats better than most people, but that didn't include herself, Leah or Fannie. They were truly his family now. "We're going to need fifty new goats if we expand into cheese making. Are you sure you want to do that?"

"Fannie knows what she's doing. You have to admit she's made some fine cheeses. If she thinks we can find an organic market, I'm willing to give it a shot."

"She's worried she'll disappoint you."

"I'll make sure she knows my love isn't tied to any success or failure. It's always there."

Anne kissed him on the cheek. "I love you."

"So you've told me."

"I haven't told you today."

"You did. Before breakfast, during milking, after milking and after lunch. Four times today, five counting right now."

"You're counting how many times I tell you that I love you?"

He pulled her close to him. "Every one. I want to remember them all."

Cupping his face between her hands, she gave him a quick peck on the lips. "I only count your kisses."

He chuckled. "How many are we up to?"

"Two thousand and seventy-one."

"No wonder my lips are tired." She swatted his shoulder and stepped away, but inside, she was smiling.

He looked over the pasture. "I'm glad we are done birthing for the year."

Was this the right time? Maybe it was the best time. "Actually, we aren't done."

"*Ja*, Fannie will have her new baby in June and then we will be done."

"There will be one more. On about October 22, by my calculations."

She watched his face. Understanding suddenly dawned on him. "You? We? Us? We're pregnant?"

She nodded. "We are. Are you happy?"

He pulled her close. "You have no idea how happy you have made me. *Gott es goot.*"

"*Ja*, He is." She closed her eyes and collected kisses number two thousand and seventy-two, seventy-three and seventy-four.

After that, she lost count as his love swept

her away to gorgeous bliss surrounded by the fragrance of honeysuckle on a green hillside of Pennsylvania overlooking her home.

* * * * *

Dear Reader,

I hope you have enjoyed the Lancaster Court-ships series. It isn't always fun to work with other writers on a project. However, I have to say that Emma Miller and Rebecca Kertz were true professionals and a joy to work with. Our editor, Melissa Endlich, did a great job of keeping us on the straight and narrow to produce a true trilogy that tied up all the stories without shortchanging any of them. No small feat.

I had to do a lot of research for this book. I'd already done quite a bit on midwives for another book, but pumpkins and goats were not something I was familiar with. For this I turned to my family. My oldest brother, Greg, and his wife, Theresa, were a wealth of information about running a small business and growing pumpkins. I love their white ones and enjoy decorating my home for fall with their produce.

For information on goats, my brother Bob hooked me up with his girlfriend, Te'Coa, a woman who runs a goat dairy and is a well-known dairy goat judge. She answered my every question and even let me watch her milk a goat. It's a pretty amazing business. Thanks to all of them, I managed to write a story I hope is mostly accurate. Any mistakes made are completely my own and not due to my resources. (Love you guys.)

I'd like to wish everyone a blessed holiday season. May your Thanksgiving, Christmas and New Year's celebrations hold true to Amish values by bringing you closer to God, family and friends.

Happy Holidays,

Patricia Davids

LARGER-PRINT BOOKS!

GET 2 FREE LARGER-PRINT NOVELS PLUS 2 FREE MYSTERY GIFTS

Love Inspired®

SUSPENSE

RIVETING INSPIRATIONAL ROMANCE

Larger-print novels are now available...

LISLP15

REQUEST YOUR FREE BOOKS!

2 FREE WHOLESOME ROMANCE NOVELS IN LARGER PRINT

PLUS 2 FREE MYSTERY GIFTS

✳✳✳✳✳✳✳✳✳✳✳✳✳✳✳✳✳✳✳✳✳✳✳✳✳

HEARTWARMING™
✾✾✾✾✾✾✾✾✾✾✾✾✾✾✾✾✾✾✾✾✾✾✾✾✾

Wholesome, tender romances

YES! Please send me **The Montana Mavericks Collection** in Larger Print. This collection begins with 3 FREE books and 2 FREE gifts (gifts valued at approx. $20.00 retail) in the first shipment, along with the other first 4 books from the collection! If I do not cancel, I will receive 8 monthly shipments until I have the entire 51-book Montana Mavericks collection. I will receive 2 or 3 FREE books in each shipment and I will pay just $4.99 US/ $5.89 CDN for each of the other four books in each shipment, plus $2.99 for shipping and handling per shipment.*If I decide to keep the entire collection, I'll have paid for only 32 books, because 19 books are FREE! I understand that accepting the 3 free books and gifts places me under no obligation to buy anything. I can always return a shipment and cancel at any time. My free books and gifts are mine to keep no matter what I decide.

263 HCN 2404   463 HCN 2404

Name _____ (PLEASE PRINT) _____

Address _____ Apt. # _____

City _____ State/Prov. _____ Zip/Postal Code _____

Signature (if under 18, a parent or guardian must sign)

Mail to the **Reader Service:**
IN U.S.A.: P.O. Box 1867, Buffalo, NY 14240-1867
IN CANADA: P.O. Box 609, Fort Erie, Ontario L2A 5X3